THE MAGIC PAINTBRUSH

The Books of 9 & 10 Penance: 1/10th

By

J. E. Krueger

Edited by George Plotkin

An imprint of Alms House, *a publishing company*
Artwork & Design by J. E. KRUEGER
1ˢᵗ edition Copyright 2012 Copyright 2022
All rights reserved. This book, or parts thereof may not be reproduced without authors expressed written permission

For

The Alchemist

ENJOY THE ART SHOW

Jay B Krueger

The magic
is
within you

*Dedicated to my father Richard Krueger and my
Uncle Greg Frederickson
For whom this book would not be possible*

CONTENTS

I The Man Inside the Painting   7

II The Year Was 1444   17

III Starry Night   29

IV The Island of Lost Dreams   41

V The Apprentice   61

VI Cradling Wheat   75

VII The King's New Castle   83

VIII Fragonard's Dream *In the Garden of Rococo*   99

IX The King's Portrait   113

X The Madness of King Fragonard   125

XI Dancer's in Blue   141

XII The Desperate Man   149

XIII The Boy Blue   157

XIV Portrait of an Artisan   173

XV Off Valparaiso   187

XVI Sunflowers   201

XVII The Algebraic Equation of a Madman   207

XVIII The Masters Duel   223

I

THE MAN INSIDE THE PAINTING

In the Holbein Museum of Fine Art where nothing interesting ever happened and no one ever had anything interesting to say, an inquisitive young boy wandered from room to room. He rarely passed another living soul. Those he did pass didn't seem to notice him at all. They were too busy talking at a whisper to the paintings hanging on the walls. It's important for them to use as many dull and boring words possible to discuss the dull and boring art. Because that's what you do in an art museum. That's how you enjoy fine art.

Occasionally, someone will shout, "Absolutely exquisite!" in a high pitched squeal. This type of behavior is not to be tolerated. Excitement is never allowed in the museum *Under! Any! Circumstances!* You are to stare at the paintings, discuss their finer points and what you find overall to be lacking.

This is the objective of the critic or the snob, to point out the faults and the flaws in the artists work as they meander on a penitential pilgrimage to dissect painting after painting until there is nothing left but an objectionable opinion. Thankfully, the young boy went fairly unnoticed by these connoisseurs of fine art gasping and gawking at the paintings.

That is, until his eyes focused in on a portrait of a young man unknown to him and the rest of the world. Certainly, there were paintings far more impressive in the museum. One's with a little more panache and ambiance and other big and confusing words to go with them. He could have picked from any number of names that are terribly difficult to pronounce, from Ter Borch to Van Eyck to Hogarth, names that leave a cough in your throat.

This painting however did something unusual. It spoke to him and not the other way around. Yet it had no signature tied to the work. Therefore, there was no reason to spend a great length of time discussing the finer points attributed to some forgotten artistic ghost of the past.

The young boy must have spent over an hour quietly enjoying the painting as one should do, when a stranger, well educated in fine art and the works housed in the museum, brushed up against his shoulder. The young boy stood back to allow the stranger to pass.

The stranger, however, felt he should inform the youth where the valued, treasured works of art are kept.

"The paintings in this room are just portraits of old men and the art they produced. Why don't you go downstairs kid and take in a modern art exhibit?" The stranger gruffly said, holding onto his broom.

"Oh no. I like it up here. They keep the best stuff on the second floor." The young boy replied with an unappreciated opinion of his own.

The stranger set his broom against the wall as he leaned closer to the painting, his eyes inches from the canvas.

"Hey kid, who is he anyways? The peasant boy in the painting."

"I'm not sure? There's no signature. Nothing to attribute this..."

"Huh. Interesting fact. All I know about art is ducks land and geese take off in these things. Never been much of a portrait lover."

"Well, there's more to it than that. For instance, this painting, despite its flaws..."

"Yeah, okay. Whatever. The museum will be closing shortly and I've got a job to do. So hurry up."

The janitor, having clarified his point about the importance of fine art, pushed his broom across the floor and vanished down the stairs.

The young boy was all alone with the paintings on the second floor. Most of the day was gone. Tired, he sat down on a bench and began to daydream with his head in his hand.

Hours later, he woke to the sound of a man speaking in a strange poetic verse. "Hello over there, are you awake?"

The young boy got up and looked around the empty room. He thought at first he was still dreaming, but then he heard the strange voice again.

"I can't see you with the view I have of this room."

"Who's there?" the young boy replied to the dull and boring art.

"Ah yes, it appears this old soul has finally grabbed your attention. I couldn't help but notice you earlier wandering around this room in one great big circle with your hands resting behind you."

"I uh, well you see. I like art and - hey, you talk kinda funny."

"So do you. Now why have you been wandering the frigid hallways of this museum, speaking to yourself and no one else for that matter?"

"I like to look at the paintings. They inspire me. Say, where are you?"

"I'm in the far corner of the room." the voice replied cheeringly with a drawn-out echo.

The young boy looked around the room again, but he still couldn't see anyone, nor find the source of that drawn-out echo bouncing off the walls of the museum.

"All I see is a painting of some sunflowers and an empty field by Millet."

"Quit wasting time on a clock that only ticks one way. I'm over here, by the Millet."

The young boy got up and went searching for the peculiar voice that insisted on speaking with him. He was sure he was the only one standing in the room, until he looked deeply into the eyes of a portrait of a man covered in dust and cobwebs.

It was a foolish thought, but the young boy had to ask, "Hello, are you real?"

"No, no, over here. Turn around. That's just old Holbein. I assure you, there is nothing to be gained by staring in depth into his dusty old eyes. I wish I would have painted his portrait myself. It's not the greatest likeness, but you get the gist of his brow."

The young boy turned around to the sight of the full-sized portrait he'd passed by many times before, only something was off. The peasant boy in the painting was moving freely as if alive, but bound by the oily textures on the canvas.

"Don't just stand there giving me looks as though I am a ghost. Introduce yourself." The boy in the painting pertinently demanded.

The young boy marveled at the painting in disbelief, unable to speak a word.

"You seem a bit perplexed. I suppose I should explain myself."

"Yes, please do." The young boy stuttered as he backed away from the painting.

12

The boy in the painting cleared the oils in his throat, "I believe you told that person earlier you did not know the name of the man that stands before you today trapped inside of a painting for all eternity."

"Well no, I guess not."

"My name is Ayden, prince and heir to the throne of the Kingdom of Fragonard. From now on when you address the next uninterested art enthusiast you will be able to give my name and proper title."

The young boy gathered his thoughts and tried shaking the dream from his head, but it was all too real.

"You're uh... a talking painting?" he said, utterly amazed.

"Why yes – I know. Now who are you?"

"My name is Stefan Vermeer and the museum will be closing shortly."

"Interesting fact Stefan, but the museum has already closed for the night. We're the only ones left, you and I. Besides, hardly anyone comes up to the second floor, unless they get lost and meander off."

"I can't believe it. How do you live in there?"

The boy in the painting rolled his eyes, "That's not important. Tell me, what do you like to do, other than sleeping in the corner of the room?"

"There's a bench over there. I was just taking a nap. I didn't mean to fall asleep."

"Alright, no reason to make a fuss. I just wanted to know why you've been viewing these paintings so attentively? I've been watching you pass by me all day."

"I'm an artist, but I lost the inspiration to paint. That's why I came to the museum."

"You're a fellow artist then. Why didn't you say so. I'm glad we have something in common of interest. So you've lost the inspiration to paint, you say? You're probably just going through a phase. I've gone through many in my lifetime. I'm sure it will pass."

"I hope so. It's just that I want to be a painter someday, but my father says it's a waste of time. He thinks I should grow up and do something more practical."

"Ah, now I see. Much like the tale of how I became the portrait of the man you see before you."

"Really, how so?"

"If you had the time, I could tell you a tale that might help you with a dream your father just doesn't understand."

Stefan shrugged his shoulders. "Sure. I suppose."

"Alright, if you suppose. Now cheer up and fetch a chair on which to sit upon. It's going to take me some time to tell you this story. Oh and if you wouldn't mind, I would appreciate it if you switched out the Millet across from me with something more suited to my tastes."

"You don't like the Millet?"

"No, it's not that. It's just that rarely do they move the paintings around in this museum. Holbein and I have been staring at it for almost a century."

"How about Starry Night by Vincent Van Gogh? It's my favorite painting in the museum."

"It does seem fitting for the story I am about to tell. Go and fetch it then, I'll wait here. Perhaps some other time I could get a chance to view some of your paintings?"

"Well that's just it. My father doesn't approve of art in the home, ever since I decided I didn't want to follow in his footsteps. So now I can't keep anything I create."

"What a shame. Hopefully you won't give up on your dreams because of this."

"I don't know. I mean what am I going to do now? I've lost the inspiration to paint and I don't know if I'll ever get it back."

"The magic is within you, I can tell. I'm sure something will come along to spark the imagination, to catch one's attention off guard. Now pull up a chair and sit down."

"Maybe you're right. So tell me this story of yours. I would like to hear how you became a painting for all eternity."

Stefan sat down on the bench with two fingers and a thumb pressed against the sides of his chin and listened to Prince Ayden's story.

"Where do I begin? Ah yes, let me see..."

II

THE YEAR WAS 1444...

...The year was fourteen forty-four. I was a young lad back then, a prince about the age of seventeen, heir to a small and poor kingdom between here and nowhere. I lived with my father in a little stone house in the center of town. He had grown quite ill over the last few years, so I had to work twice as hard to sustain myself by farming the fields in the countryside. Our kingdom was made up of mostly peasants who also worked hard, earning a living of either farming or goat herding.

Occasionally, we would adopt people from other countries that could no longer support themselves in their homeland. This made the days go by much easier for us. These people would often bring with them special skills or talents that our kingdom otherwise would have never seen, as we were so far from anywhere at all. I guess that's where my story begins. You see it was because of my father's acceptance of people from other nations that determined my fate and the fate of our entire kingdom.

It all started when I was walking back to town after a grueling day of doing chores. I encountered a group of Italians on the edge of town who recently arrived by sea. They were selling whatever luggage they carried with. "Buy this," they would say. "Try that," another would suggest. That sort of thing. It was obvious these people didn't know what long days in the fields were. The clothing they wore was finely tailored. I thought it fascinating, the things they had for sale. They had the most amazing paintings. The portraits they produced were so realistic they could've been alive. It was abundantly clear that was where their skills lay.

One of the men was in the midst of painting one of these magnificent portraits when I walked up to talk to him. He wore fine black attire and an odd looking long and billowy hat. I introduced myself to him as Prince Ayden of the hardworking kingdom of Fragonard. I exclaimed that he could stay here for as long as he liked, so long as he like to farm or raise goats.

He lifted his brow and replied, "Ah, but I like to create art with my hands. Perhaps his royal highness could use a painter in the King's royal court?"

I brushed some dirt off my shoulder and said, "I'm afraid our kingdom can't afford a painter and the king's royal court that you speak of. It is nothing more than a dirt road running though the center of town."

It was a pity, he told me. To never know of the arts. He then introduced himself as Jared Botticelli of Italy and told me of his troubles finding suitable work. I felt sorry for this poor old man, knowing he would never get paid full value for his talents around here. So I asked if he would care to join me and my father for supper and a place to rest until he figured things out. He accepted my invitation and offered to paint my father's portrait in return for my kindness. I thought what a wonderful gesture, so we gathered up his things and walked to my father's home in the center of town.

My father looked over some of his paintings and agreed. It was a true shame to waste this man's talents, but we just couldn't afford a painter. Then I told him our new friend would paint a portrait of him in exchange for a place to stay until he landed back on his feet. My father was thrilled at the idea of having his likeness captured on the canvas. He said he could stay as long as he needed to paint his portrait.

The next day I decided to take the painter down the main road of town to where the skilled craftsmen sold things our people could not do without. It was my hope he would find work amongst them, as he was clearly not fit for the backbreaking efforts it took to farm our dusty fields.

We first stopped by Logan Landseer's, the local blacksmith to see if he needed any help with trimming hooves. He was a rough and gruff sort. The pay was good, but the hours were long and dreadful. I helped him out one summer a few years back. It wasn't something I planned on doing again myself anytime soon. I've still got the knots in my hands from it.

My new friend didn't think he could put up the heat coming from the furnace, so on we went to Renoir's, the town tailor. He was always on the lookout for a good button sower or someone who didn't mind getting their hands dirty washing clothes. Botticelli felt such laborious duties were beneath him. I assume wherever he was from, the standard of living he was accustomed too was more than our people could afford or even dream of for that matter.

We walked up and down the main road all morning, but I couldn't find anything that interested him. Then we stopped by the local bakery run by Enstrom and his daughter Rhoda. I invited him inside for lunch. After he was done slurping down a bowl of soup, I asked if he would like working for him, since he enjoyed slopping his bread in the broth so much.

He replied with distain, "My skills would be wasted on such a menial task performed for the everyday life of the people. Besides, with my talents I'm sure there's work elsewhere more suited for me."

I realized it was going to take some effort to get him and the rest of the Italians accustom to our simple way of living. He just had no understanding of servitude. He then asked why I didn't just merely take the bread from tax since I was a prince.

I replied confidently, "Those who work hard for their efforts truly get to enjoy the fruits of their labors."

This was a creed by which our people swore by, something my father told me a long time ago. He agreed and said although he'd never heard anything like this, it truly was a motto on which to live ones life.

At the end of our tour through town Botticelli asked if there was any work I could find him that didn't involve manual labor. We were a stoic society, built on the foundation of working hard for ones efforts and there was no getting around it. I myself, the King's son couldn't even avoid the work that needed to be done in the fields. So I told him he better get used to it if he wanted to stay here.

He replied in a humble manner, "If you were, however, to have a place big enough or perhaps a castle with servant's quarters and stables, then could I be the Royal Painter?"

I shook my head and said, "You truly are a dreamer, but what would my people do to pay for all of this? If all we have is enough to farm for ourselves."

That conversation would prove to be both a blessing and a curse for my father and our people.

Later that evening, I noticed the painter sitting outside with his head in his hand. I sat down next to him and told him it would be nice to have all those wonderful things he talked about, but that we couldn't just spend the rest of our lives idly dreaming of them. He sealed his lips in a crooked manner and let out a long sigh, as his eyes drifted towards a distant star. The painter kept ignoring me and the rest of the world.

After awhile he muttered, "Maybe we could have all those wonderful things, if only we dare to dream of them."

He truly was a dreamer Stefan, not cut out for work in the fields, but I was intrigued by this man's dreams and the way he spoke of them.

I sat with him a little while longer, then mentioned I might possibly have some work for him in the fields. Nothing too strenuous, just some menial tasks, mostly picking up rocks and sticks to help clear the field. He thought working with a prince who chose the life of a peasant might give him a new outlook and gladly took me up on my offer.

It was getting late and I'd stared at the stars long enough. So I got up and told him he could sleep on the cot by our fireplace. He said the grass and the flowers in our front yard would suit him just fine. I thought this was rather odd. He had such high standards, but I didn't think twice about it. I decided to continue the conversation another time.

The next day I gave Botticelli some of my father's old work clothes and brought him out to the fields with me. It was a small square plot of land right next to Grant Wood's farm, but enough to earn a humble living. The first chore of the day was to finish removing an old tree stump my father and I had struggled with for the past few years. Its root system an entangled mess, deeply immersed in the soil. I handed Botticelli a shovel and told him to start digging. He acted confused, as if he didn't know what to do. Clearly, he'd never worn a working man's shoe.

I told him, "That's not how you hold it. Place the handle in your hands firmly like this. Plant it into the ground and then push down with your heel. Then pull the dirt out and swing it behind you."

Seemed simple enough. It took him a few tries, but eventually he got the hang of it, though he treated the dirt on his attire like a disease ravaging his very essence. I told him not to fear the dirt, but to wear it proudly as a badge of honor for the work he put in. His lips cringed, as he wiped the dirt from the front of his shirt and started shoveling away without saying a word.

Around noon we walked over to a tree near the side of the road and sat down to have our lunch. Botticelli propped his back up against the tree and took a nap while I ate my apple. I don't think he'd ever worked this hard before. Being a field hand isn't easy by any means. The daily routine can get pretty boring, but if you were to ask me. The reward at the end of the season is well worth it in my opinion. Though somedays I really wished there was more to life then pulling weeds and tilling the earth.

When we were through with our lunch I told him we better get back to work. He folded his hat over his sights and crossed his arms. I leaned down, pushed his hat back up and told him if we were ever to finish the chores before the sun went down, we'd have to get started.

My father's old friend Grant Wood then started pulling up from down the way. He was an ornery old sort, not that easy to get along with if you didn't know him. He'd express himself through hand gestures and an occasional nod. Certainly wasn't the type to put up with sleeping on the job. So I helped Botticelli on his feet and told him to start picking rocks out of the field while I talked with him.

Grant Wood then pulled along side me and asked how I was doing with a tip of his straw hat. I wiped the sweat from my brow and nodded back as I took the last bite of my apple. That old man could tell a lot about a person just by watching them work. It didn't take long for him to eye Botticelli over and ask me what I had gotten myself into. I told him I was trying out a new worker for the season, giving him a chance at it. He rubbed his hand on his chin, paused for a moment and then grunted.

To me, that meant he was suggesting I find a replacement soon, preferably someone who could handle the weight of a shovel. I nodded back with a firm eye, letting him know not to worry. He'd get used to it, if I pushed him hard enough. Grant

25

Wood wasn't so sure, but he lifted his hat and let me deal with it on my own as he always had.

When Grant Wood left, I walked back out to the middle of the field and asked Botticelli to pick up his shovel and help me finish removing the stump. We dug our heels in deep and pried with all our might until we had it loose enough to pull it away. It was a relief to finally open up new land for planting. I couldn't wait to tell my father what my new friend and I had accomplished that morning. I knew he would be proud to know his son had done something that day we both had struggled with for the past few years.

At the end of the day I asked Botticelli if he would still be interested in doing the same type of work tomorrow. We'd be up bright and early, I promised him. He complained about the hot sun, the dirt on his clothes and the taste of it left in his mouth. He said the worst of it was the aches and pains all over his body that he'd never felt before. I chuckled and assured him after a few more days of this, things would get much easier. He sighed with a look of grief on his face and kept that expression on our walk back to town.

I offered him the cot in our home, figuring the cold hard ground wouldn't be very comforting after such grueling work. To my surprise, he turned down my offer. Instead, he lay down on his bed of grass and flowers and went to sleep.

Over the course of the next few weeks my new friend and I worked the fields together. Botticelli truly showed he could accomplish much when motivated and given a task to complete. The following week, however, proved to be a disaster. Every day I would find him asleep by noon under the shade of that tree. I tried hard finding him menial tasks to perform and I gave him much praise for his efforts, but it was of no use. I couldn't even get him to lift one small stone and remove it from the field. Maybe Grant Wood was right, but I still had faith I could make a workingman out of him yet. All it would take would be to find his niche.

28

III

STARRY NIGHT

The next week came and still I struggled to find his niche. I worked hard from sun up to sun down, while he slept comfortably in the shade under the tree next to our field. It was becoming a problem supporting someone who didn't want to work for their efforts. I realized then I had to tell him to find work elsewhere, if I was ever to catch up on my chores. Though it was a shame, because I did enjoy our conversations on the long walk back to town.

When we got home Botticelli sat down on the bench to gaze upon the stars as he often did. I asked why he stared at them every night.

He replied, "The stars are like an unreachable paradise floating idle in the sky, just waiting to be tamed by a master. Some day I would like to visit there and ride on the fat line of the crocodiles back."

Intrigued by this unusual thought, I wondered how one could venture to a place so far away and reach it? He said he might actually have the answer as he got up and began riffling through his things. I should have gone to bed, but I was curious about this answer he claimed to have tucked away somewhere.

He came back and showed me an old wooden box and a painter's palette. I told him it was far too late to paint and that there wasn't enough light to see. He laughed and wet his painter's palette anyways.

He then opened his box and pulled out a very fine and clean paintbrush and said, "Ah, but what if there was enough light? Then I would not be dreaming and then I could paint to my heart's desire."

I felt sympathetic to this poor old painter who believed the answer to all his problems were hidden amongst the stars. I sat there anyways entertaining the idea, hoping to somehow feel like a daydreamer myself for once in my plain ordinary life.

Botticelli raised his paintbrush in the air and with a stroke of inspiration, he placed a spectacular spell of bright blue colors over the sky. In an instant the stars came alive, luminous amber orbs of light twinkling in a nocturnal dream. The pigments he used were bold and dramatic. His movements were erratic and swift, as he swirled the brush over the mysterious nature of the wind, moving it in a transparent whorl. It was sorcery I thought, intertwined with his imagination yet it was the most amazing thing I'd ever seen.

With wild excitement in his eyes reflecting in my own, he said, "This is a magic paintbrush and I can do all this and more with it. So tell me, do you still think I am a dreamer young Ayden?"

I didn't reply. The only thing I did was stare in awe as he did something else with his brush you just had to see to believe. He used the stars to create a bright and brilliant stage resembling our fields. Then he turned a drifting cloud the other way, transforming it into a surreal castle floating in the air. It was a milky white daydream.

Then he placed the constellation Perseus on the stage and gave him a crown with the brightest star in the sky as the center jewel. He asked if I would like a horse, as he smirked at my enthusiasm. Of course I said yes. I had dreams too, though none were as magnificent as his.

At my request, he galloped the constellation Pegasus to where I proudly stood amongst the stars and put on a show.

Throughout the play my character slayed a beastly looking dragon with fiery eyes, the color of the sun and defeated a whispering witch of the woods. Towards the end of the show, after defeating the constellation Hydra, I blew the beautiful maiden Andromeda a kiss. Then I mounted my horse and rode into the Milky Way as he closed the curtains with a shower of teary stars. They were vibrantly lit, like sparkling jewels and brighter then the Northern Lights that shined a prism of hope over the harsh winters had in our kingdom.

The epic adventures I had up there still to this day rival any story I've heard over the past few centuries. It all took place on a stage modeled after the fields I worked so hard in. I guess that's why I remember it so fondly.

We were having the time of our lives, but it was getting late and although, I'd never stayed up long enough to truly enjoy what the heavens had to offer, I had to get to bed. The chores just weren't going to take care of themselves in the morning. Then he offered me the chance of a lifetime. He asked if I wanted to be a daydreamer too. I quickly took him up on this offer. After all, how could one refuse such a wondrous gift, to be able to move stars anyway one chooses.

He gave me the brush, his palette of paint and told me all I had to do was find a mixture of colors that blended well together. Then I could paint whatever the heart desires. At first I didn't know what to do with this magic in my hands. I'd never attempted anything like this. So I arched my wrist and carefully placed just a sliver of paint over the outer-rim of the moon to see what would happen. I couldn't believe it. It actually worked. The moon grew big and bright, radiating out in a soft mellow glow.

Written in the stars was a dream I'd never known. I was captivated by the paint and what I could do with it. There were no limitations, the moment I touched the sky and began playing with the cosmos.

I didn't hold back, I carved into the canvas of the night, using wide swatches of blue and grey. My strokes quickly got caught in a cluster of clouds and pooled under duress in the center of this masterpiece. With a quick twirling dash I released the air, swirling it in a fiery mist of white and deep shades of midnight blue. Here I was just a young farm-boy who never knew what a dream could be. It was pure magic blowing in the wind.

Then I tried to move the stars around like he did, only it proved to be a difficult challenge. They became mere streaks, shooting embers of light that broke apart and fizzled into nothing. So he offered me some advice on how to properly use the brush.

He told me to be careful when dipping it into the paint and place just enough on the ends of the bristles so it will not drip. Then choose a star on which to practice, swipe the brush across its ever glowing light and simply lift up. It was as simple as that.

With a final thought, he said, "If you allow the magic to come alive on its own, then the cosmic drama of the stars will unfold before you."

I paid close attention to his advice. It wasn't long after I got the hang of things that I was able put on a show of my own. I washed the brush back and forth, creating a thin veneer over the starry world above. Slowly but surly the surface began to glean like a mirror, reflecting the unique qualities of our village below. The world above seem to meld with this enchantment in the sky. It was as if an ocean of stars were drifting through our world below. You could see everything at a glance, even as far away as Grant Wood's farm.

For the finale to this magical performance I gathered all the stars I could find and placed them in a line. Botticelli was intrigued. He begged me to tell him what I was going to do next. I turned to him and smiled before releasing them as shower of glittery dust. Thousands of stars hurled towards the earth in a dazzling light show, only to be stopped as I whisked them away in one swift stroke. He said he'd never seen something so imaginative, but he was concerned I may have painted away his dreams. I told him not to worry, as I scattered them back across my blank canvas.

We then both had a good laugh over such a silly thing. I spent the next few hours coming up with new things to make him laugh and he did so many times that night. I was in a dream and no one could wake me, not even the bell that rang every morning, with all its might. The rest of the world though, must've been wondering what was happening to the heavens above.

After awhile he asked for his paintbrush back. He said he wanted to show me something. I handed it back to him and he wiped it clean. His eyes grew into a sparkling wonderment, as he took the tip and focused on the brightest star he could find. When the star adhered to his brush, he carefully pulled it out of the night and placed it before me.

He then said something that has always stuck with me over the years.

"The stars and moon and heavens above have always been and always will be and as great and vast as they are, sometimes we just have to look up to truly know they are there."

To this day I wonder if everything that happened that night was a mere dream, but it must have been real. Something so imaginative couldn't have come from the thoughts of a field hand. He truly had a niche, an envious skill with which no one could match in their wildest of dreams.

The night was coming to a close, so he asked if I would join him next to his bed of grass and flowers. We got up and he painted the flowers to health, as they had been broken by his back when he slept on them. He painted a bed of my own next to his and then we laid down to watch as he put the stars in their rightful place. I still wonder how he knew exactly where to place each one and if some of the constellations he didn't create on his own. I can only assume it was from many long nights spent gazing at them, because he played with them with such ease.

After the stars were in their proper place, he handed me the brush and told me to paint the moon back to its normal silvery hue, only with the laughter we shared. I really had no idea how to blend and mix colors together back then. He said no matter, paint it any hue you like. I rather liked that idea, the freedom to create what I wanted without the intuition of another getting in the way.

When I swiped the smile across the face of the moon, laying the final stroke over this masterpiece sculpted out of my first dream, he said he would leave it unchanged forever, so that we would always remember the laughter and magic we shared. I agreed we leave it alone. It felt fitting at the time and as far as I know the moon is still holding onto the laughter we relished in on that magical *Starry Night.*

The stars soon thereafter faded and I quickly went to sleep beside him to the sound of a bell ringing in the distance. My eyes could no longer stay open. I was too tired to realize it was the early morning bell, waking anyone whom did not waste their time daydreaming the night away.

The next day I woke to my father standing over me with a disapproving glare.

"What time is it father?" I muttered.

"It's almost noon and here I find you asleep in front of my home. When are the two of you planning on going to work?"

I quickly got on my feet and tried to explain, "I'm sorry father, I forgot. It's just that I was up late."

"Son, I can't afford having you spend all your free time with every drifter that wanders through town. There's work to be done."

37

I apologized again to my father, as Botticelli still lay there sleeping in content with his dreams. My father told me to wake up my new friend and have him help out, if I ever planned on finishing the chores. I tried waking him, but he didn't want to get up. It was obvious, all he wanted to do was sleep on his bed of grass and flowers. So my father grabbed a pail of water and threw it on his face. Botticelli jumped to his feet and without saying a word, followed me on my walk to start the day.

When we made it to the fields Botticelli walked over to the tree and fell asleep as he usually did. I picked up a shovel and stuck it into the first layer of soil. The chores were a struggle for once. I often took breaks to gather enough strength for even the most menial of tasks. I'd never felt so lazy and useless. The sun had almost vanished when I was finally done. I woke Botticelli and told him it was time to leave. He looked at me in a daze, as if he wanted to go back to sleep. Reluctantly, he made his way on his feet.

On the way home I remembered everything that transpired the night before and asked if any of it was real.

He eagerly replied, "Oh yes, it was all quite real, but if I am to show you again I'll need plenty of sleep, so that my mind can wander and dream of such wonderful and vivid sights."

I asked where he obtained his magical paintbrush that did these amazing things to the nighttime sky. So we took a break on our walk home and he told me his story.

40

IV

THE ISLAND OF LOST DREAMS

My story begins a very long time ago. Far from Italy, far from your village. You see, I had a father like yours once. He was always pushing me to work harder. If only he could've understood that my dreams were going to lead me to much success beyond his farthest expectations. Then maybe he wouldn't have pushed me so hard. I guess you could say the brush and I were destined to be because of my dreams.

Someday you Prince Ayden will have to choose between the life your father has destined for you to live or a life of your own, perhaps one as a painter such as myself.

When I became of age I left home never to return to pursue those dreams. I wandered the countryside as a nomad searching for the answer. Then one day, as I was looking for a place to take a nap I stumbled upon a dark and mysterious woods. It was enchanting, almost calling my name, compelling me to explore further. I opened the magical door so to speak and went deep into the forest down a well-worn trail. The path led me to an open field in the middle of nowhere. From there I went up and over a hill and then up and over another, casting a shadow over the one I left behind.

There at the top I found a place where I could put my troubled thoughts to rest next to an old and lonely tree. I lay down in its heel and waited for the stars to appear. Hours later I woke in a dream floating alongside the clouds, as if though I were one myself. I drifted along, until I landed on a desolate beach. The sands sparkled and glistened, spiraling infinitely in a rainbow effect. I couldn't even begin to describe with words how beautiful it was. So I smiled and laughed for no reason as I turned and looked out into the ocean.

I was hypnotized by the rhythmic nature of the waves, unaware the next wonderment on this island of lost dreams would be a hellish nightmare. The waters rushing in were black and oily. It didn't smell like the salt in the air as it should, but of fear and old burnt wood. I stepped back from this strange foul odor and looked into its depths with a new, perspective eye. I could see horrific dreams transpiring in the lapping waves, growing with intensity stroke after stroke. It was so terrifying, like a violent scream that never ended. I promised myself to never speak aloud of what I saw.

I had to get away, the waters were putting a strain on my eyes. I began making my way along the shoreline, searching for the cause of this dream. Giant rock cliffs lined the beach. They had these haunting images embedded in them. I thought they were purposely misleading me on. Then the beach opened up to an inlet cove. It was so unbelievably blue. The contrast against the night and the dark waves made it appear as if it had this effervescent glow. There was no where else to go and an islands shore can only lead to one place, once it's been explored. So I swam across to the other side and continued walking.

Just outside of the shadows in the next bend I heard this exotic laughter. I turned the corner and saw the most unusual creatures, tanned red skin and dark faces gathered around a fire, lit ablaze by thousands of shades of color streaming into the air. I sat down, keeping my distance and watched as they played a peculiar guessing game. These creatures were trying to catch one of the flames, being careful to capture a specific one of their choosing. When they caught one that eyed their fancy, they would hold it in the palm of their hand and present it before the others. Then, after everyone had a look they would gently blow on it, sending it afloat into the night as a dancing creature of another design.

For a brief moment I swore one of them saw me. The creature glared in suspicion as if I was a trespasser. I cautiously took a few steps forward, hoping somehow to let them know I was only curious about their game. The creature became enraged by my presence, thrashing its head violently. It crushed the burning ember in its claw like hand. The ember turned to graduals of sand sifting through its fingers. I knew at that moment I was not meant to see this game of theirs. Though I wanted to let them know I meant no harm, there was no way of telling them with words I assumed they couldn't understand.

Then an unsettled wave pushed forward and washed over the fire. The creatures scattered down the beach in a cloud of black smoke. When the haze vanished, all I could see was a spot glowing in the distance where their fire used to be. I can only assume they were more scared of me than I of them. I thought perhaps because the waves were coming in to close to shore and they feared that is where I may have come from.

What was left of their game were just a few dwindling flames in a pile of hot coals and ash. I walked over and dipped my hand in to see if I could catch a small flame. I was able to pull out a green ember the size of a pebble, lit with a fading hope. I blew on it, hoping to get my chance to play along, but the flame drifted away as nothing more than a memory of what I'd seen. I tried a few more times, yet still I could not join in and soon thereafter, what was left of their fire grew cold.

With nothing to keep me amused, I decided to see what other wondrous things awaited me in this dream of dreams, just in case I woke up. I continued further down the beach until I found a pathway that led inland through the dense brush. The path took me up and over a hill and then up and over another. There at the top was a tree just like the one in the forest. Next to the tree I noticed a stick wedged into the ground. It had a worn handle, aged well by the years of its use. I assumed someone else must have walked this path before I did and left it there. It all of a sudden occurred to me. I'd seen this place once, a long time ago in a dream I had when I was a small child. That's when I felt at home, like I truly belonged on this island, more than I will ever know.

It twas a land beyond, beyond, a place past hope and fear where only dreamers dare to exist far from all that we wish to know and comprehend. The stars never seemed so bright and amazing in all my life spent gazing at them. They danced and played a game of their own in a spectacular show of colors, just like the flames from the fire. It was then that I realized my destiny lay beyond them, the magnificent stars in all their glory.

I will say this. In all my attempts to recreate this persistent memory, last night when you and I played with the cosmos tempting fate to see what we could find, it was the closest I'd ever been to obtaining my dreams.

I propped my back up against the tree to rest for awhile and enjoy all I had discovered. Just as I was about to close my eyes a flower landed on my nose. I couldn't believe what I was seeing. This mysterious flower opened its pedals and fluttered away, as if though it were a butterfly. Intrigued, I pulled the walking stick out of the ground and followed after as it glided over the valley below.

There were droves of these eloquently lit flowers nesting in a field of tall curling grasses that were intricately woven together in a patchwork of dark hues. I felt a sudden gush of wind. In an instant the peaceful meadow turned into a rage of animated colors, swaying sharply from light to dark in flickering movements. The flowers broke free from their stems and flew in a haze of wild, vivid dreams sparkling before me. After the winds died down, they landed back on their stems and went to sleep.

It was such a marvelous sight that I often look back on this dream and wonder if my eyes were playing tricks on me. It must have been real though. Something like this couldn't have possibly come from the thoughts of someone who never dared to dream beyond all they knew as reality.

On the other side of the valley was a thick groove of trees, as strange and beautiful as those flowers. They had this surrealistic dream like quality. I put the walking stick out in front and traversed my way through the forest down a red and blue stream. There were these bubbling pools of creamy pastelic mauves all over the forest floor. It saturated the tree bark, causing a rainbow effect to twirl upward.

The path began to wind down as the stream dissipated over an open field. I saw the most beautiful thing of all in the middle. It was a horse like no other, leaned over, taking a quiet drink from a purple lake. It had a gorgeous black mane that flowed endlessly into the night. The most wonderful hues were shaded in on its back. There was red and green, blue and pink and orange. Oh and I'll never forget its eyes. They were a striking cadmium yellow, unyieldingly vibrant and powerful.

With nowhere else to go as I'd found the place I was searching for, I sat down on a stone near the lake to ponder on the mystical qualities of this horse, bound in legend and myth. The stone acted startled and then it stood up and walked away, knocking me to the ground. While I was brushing myself off an odd looking creature stepped out of the shadows. It was very similar to the ones on the beach, only with more human like attributes. At first I was afraid, but my fears were settled when this creature spoke.

We had quite an interesting conversation next to that lake. The first thing the creature told me was the stone I sat upon had not been tossed or thrown, nor tipped or turned on its side, nor split or chipped nor broken in two or moved from its spot since the beginning of time.

I immediately apologized for sitting on the stone. I didn't mean to cause it to move from its spot, since it hadn't been moved for such a long time. The creature asked why I would apologize, since the stone to it did not appear to be disturbed in any way. I thought to myself what an odd point of view, but then I remembered the many eccentric painters I once knew from my travels and the words this thing spoke made sense.

I asked the creature if any of this was real or if I was merely trapped in a dream. Our conversation became deep and philosophical.

The creature bowed its head and replied, "Yes, you are in a dream, but not just any. This is a dream of a dream."

I then asked the creature why I was brought to the island. It explained that only the utmost creative thinkers could visit there and that I must be one of them. I asked if this were true, I just couldn't fathom that I could be equal to something so pure and full of joy. It replied yes, along with the flowers, the trees, the butterflies, the blades of grass and everything else I encountered. I then asked how this island came to be.

The creature spoke in an inquisitive manner, as it replied with a questionable, yet reasoning sense.

"Why you are a daydreamer, is it so hard to believe a place like this could exist?"

It should have seemed so obvious to me. Of course a place like this could exist, if only we dare to dream of it. I then asked how to leave this enchanting place. The creature was befuddled. It wondered why I would ever want wake up from such a peaceful memory. But it told me that if I really wanted to leave, I had the answer all along. I should have already known, all I had to do was daydream the day away once more.

The creature then asked if I wanted to stay. I said I would think about it, but that there was still so much out in the world to see.

It simply replied, "Everything you will ever see for the rest of your life could never compare to this beautiful place. The things on this island, you will never see ever again if you choose to leave."

I couldn't have agreed more with this strange looking creature I was conversing with in such an odd manner. I then told the creature of my walk through the island and the game I saw the others playing on the beach. I asked why they wouldn't let me join in. It said I was not yet one of them. To play as freely on the island as they did would require a new face. I then asked about the ocean, why it was black and filled with such vile turbulence in its darkened waves.

The creature replied in a grim voice with a cautious, warning sense.

"Do not go near the waters surrounding the island. They are dead and filled with horrific nightmares, the worst ever conceived by mortal man. If you stare into the depths of this briny malevolent evil for too long, they will consume you. Then you will be lost in a place of misery, forgotten and remembered as nothing more than a dream of your world and of this island."

We made light conversation for a while and then it said I only had until daylight to decide if I wanted to stay. I was told when day broke the island would disappear and I would never be able to return. Though I wasn't sure if I wanted to stay and leave my reality behind, I asked how I could become a part of this beautiful place.

The creature raised its head toward a shooting star breaking apart in the sky and said, "To enter a dream you must first become a dream."

It also told me that if I decided to stay, all I would have to do is drink from the mystical purple lake. Then fall asleep in the field of flowers atop the great hill, the one standing just outside of another's dream and daydream a creature of my own mystical design. That was how all the creatures ended up permanently staying on the island.

I wondered at that point if this creature was not once a man. So I asked what I thought it would reply with another easily understood question to some and for others, an impossible dream.

The creature told me, "I was once a man by the name of Albert Moore and I came here after a dream I had one summer night the year before."

I asked the creature if it had another name. It told me the horse had given him the name Izoozo, after a great tree that used to sing this mystical place to sleep before the sun came up. I was told those were the dark days of the island.

I then asked if even the horse was once a man. The creature said something intriguing that I still don't fully understand.

"No, the horse was here long before any of us. It is the lifeblood and creator of paradise everlasting. The inhabitants here revere and admire it more than anything that you have encountered in this dream."

I thought everything the creature was telling me was so intriguing that I often think of the conversation we had and wished I had chosen to stay. The creature then left me alone for the rest of the night to ponder on my decision.

I sat by the lake, looking at this horse, wondering what powers it held and where it truly came from, but I couldn't spend all my time pondering on the impossible. I knew morning would be approaching soon, so I had to make up my mind and fast or wake up. I decided to take one last stroll around the island to contemplate on whether to stay or leave and become nothing more than a forgotten memory of this dream of dreams.

On my walk I truly started to notice how everything on the island was breathing as if alive. Even the blades of grass had a place and a life of their own in this enchanting dream. Although, I wondered why what was once a man chose a new life

52

so small and insignificant. The stone I sat upon earlier then wandered by. It too was breathing as if alive. That's when I realized I couldn't have moved it, because it had legs and could do that on its own.

It was nearing early dawn and I truly felt paradise had nothing more to offer me. So I decided to say my goodbyes to the horse. I approached the creature from behind, as not to disturb its peaceful ways. The horse, for a brief moment turned to its side, then went back to munching on some of that strange curling grass. I quickly ducked below a patch of willow reeds and looked through the winding blades. I remained hidden amongst the bugs and worms that fed upon their earthly roots, observing this mystical creature, this King of dreams when its long black mane floated near me.

I wondered if the horse wouldn't mind if I sampled just a lock of hair, as a memory of my own of this place, since I would be leaving in the morning. I looked around for something sharp and found a stone, content with its place in paradise. When the horse's mane waved in front of me again, I grabbed hold and quickly cut a small sample. The horse turned around and stared directly at me. Its eyes were glowing in fiery shades of yellow. Like a lighting bolt it turned into something else darker then the ocean surrounding the island.

This new creature began huffing and puffing, kicking up dust. So I put the lock of hair into my pocket for safe keeping, then I took a few steps back. I accidently tripped over a tree stump and fell, spraining my ankle. I wondered if the stump was the one they called Izoozo, the one that used to sing this place to sleep before the sun came up. The creature then swiftly ran passed, vanishing into a cloud of nothing.

The perfect dream I'd happily found myself lost in was spinning out of control. The peaceful inhabitants started chasing after me. Even the butterfly flowers and the stone, it leapt into the air, desperately trying to knock me unconscious, split me in two and turn me into one of their foreboding dreams.

With the help of the walking stick I was able to make my way atop the two hills. I stuck it in the ground and left it for another to help navigate their way. The heavens I once admired were torn apart. The three moons had collided into each other and the stars were falling away from the sky in a shower of hell fire and rain. It seemed this world was on the verge of dying, ready to have its final dream and wake up, perhaps for all eternity.

I went down by the beach to look for an escape. The creature's I encountered earlier were waiting there for me. Their fire had been relit. I could see it in their eyes, the rage they had against me. I got down on my knees and prayed I would wake up.

Thank the stars and moon above my prayers were answered. The sun began to slowly rise, showering me with its golden rays of salvation. The islands colors faded, becoming less and less vivid as I rose into the sky and once again became one with the clouds. I floated along well into the day, until I landed back in the field from where I dreamed this dream of dreams.

When I awoke from my dream it was night. I thought none of this could have been real just as you thought once, but then I remembered the lock of hair I took from the horse. So I reached into my pocket. It was still there. After I made it back home to Italy I had the lock of hair turned into a paintbrush. I was afraid to use it and I guess what I feared the most was unlocking the nightmare I'd experienced on the island and releasing it upon the world.

Then late one evening, as I was looking for a place to rest in the woods on the edge of town, I unlocked its secrets out of boredom. The air was saturated in a heavy mist, not unlike the island, only void of a dreamers dream. I painted a flower into one of those mysterious butterflies. To my amazement, the flower began to sway with the wind, as if struggling for life to happen. It then broke free from its stem and fluttered away into the distance. I wondered, if it was a haunting illusion or if indeed this was real.

Ever since then that is why I prefer to sleep outdoors, so that I may rest on a bed made of this dream of dreams, impossible for those who do not wish to dare beyond all they know as reality.

The next day I returned to the place I was visiting. I found the town in ruins and the butterflies and the other wonderful things I brought to life lying dead in the streets. The town was in fear of my newfound magic and searching for the cause. I left, fearing I would be discovered as the perpetrator of this great tragedy that had befallen on their humble little village by standards. I realized after that day it would take quite some time to truly unlock and master the skills of this brush.

"Well, my new friend, prince and heir to a poor kingdom, what did you think of my story?"

I thought it was the most amazing story I'd ever heard. I asked if he would teach me how to paint and how I could become a daydreamer like him. He said we could start learning this magical skill tomorrow if I like. I jumped at the chance. After all, how could one refuse such an amazing gift? He said instead of taking him to work in the fields, we should find a suitable place for us to comfortably sleep the day away, perhaps under that tree by the side of the road. I laughed and said my father would never allow this type of behavior. There were just too many chores that always needed to get done. He said if we were, however, to spend the day dreaming, perhaps I would never have to do chores ever again.

What a foolish thought it was, but I was so intrigued by this idea it made me wonder if it were possible for once to live a life of ease in our hardworking kingdom. It was getting late and I was sure we would miss supper, so we walked back to my father's humble little home.

My father was waiting for me with a cold plate of food set at the table. He asked if I was planning on taking the drifter outside with me to work, since he seemed to be the source of my troubles lately. I assured him I'd make a working man out of him yet.

My father scoffed and said, "Do not to defend or waste my time with those who cannot take a blessing with gratitude."

"Please father. Give him one more chance. I need the help." I desperately pleaded.

"He's your problem for now, but if it takes more than a week I will not feed him from my table nor allow him to sleep so comfortably in our front yard. Is that understood?"

"You have my word. If things don't workout by weeks end, I'll tell him myself to leave."

"You better or you'll find yourself sleeping outdoors with him from now on."

After my father calmed down and went to bed, I went outside to see if Botticelli would show me some of his works of art, in hopes he had a painting of this mythical place. He riffled through his things, but all he really had were portraits of old men. Then I noticed the unfinished portrait I saw him working on when we first met. I asked if this was his father, he took such care of it. He quietly said no, it was a portrait of a man from the last place he visited who was very kind to him. He gave him a place to stay and allowed him to sleep on the flowers in his backyard.

Botticelli's sleeve then pulled away from his arm, as he was lifting the portrait up to admire it. I noticed a tattoo of a dragon with red and green, blue and pink and orange scales. It had these distinct yellow eyes and a black tale that wrapped around his arm almost endlessly in a hypnotic whorl. I wondered if this was what the horse turned into when he clipped the hair from its mane. So I asked if he painted it on his arm as a reminder of that night. He reacted in a rather snide way, as if he was bothered by this question. He exclaimed that he received the tattoo from a friend of his long before he acquired the brush. I then asked he tell me more of his travels. He curled his lips together in an upward lifting manner and told me he would save those stories for another time.

It was getting late and I was sure we would have many nights for him to tell me that story and many more I'm sure he had from his years of traveling and looking for a dream he never truly found. So I let him be to sleep the night away on his bed of dreams, perhaps thinking of that mythical place he once visited.

V

THE APPRENTICE

After hearing his story all I could think about was learning how to become a painter like him. The only problem was my father made it very clear, if I couldn't get him to pitch in and lend a hand, then he had to leave. Maybe old Grant Wood was right after all, he just wasn't cut out for this type of work.

So the next morning I told him if he didn't give it some effort and at least try, my father wasn't going to allow him to sleep in our front yard anymore. He assured me this was his day to prove his worth, though I had my doubts.

We walked out to the countryside and I assumed he planned on sleeping underneath the shade of that tree as usual. Instead, he stood right alongside me and asked where we should get started.

I dug my back into the first layer of soil and said, "If you really want to help, then you could pick up a plough and get that row ready for planting seed."

Botticelli yawned and said, "I thought you wanted to learn how to become a painter like me?"

I replied, "I do, but as long as there are chores to be done, then there will be no time for such foolish nonsense. Now pick up a plough and do something useful." as I dug my back into yet another layer of soil.

Botticelli, ever persistent suggested, "Ah, but why bother with such labor intensive duties, when we have our dreams safely tucked away in a wooden box?"

I turned with a tainted brow and said, "Alright then, how do you suppose we till the earth and plant the crops, if not with our backs driven deep into the soil?"

He pulled out his paintbrush and palette and then he painted a delicious red apple out of thin air and said,

"If only you'd learn, a daydreamer doesn't have to spend their whole day breaking their back, when all they have to do is simply paint what desires lay hidden from view."

I was in awe with his skill as he handed me the apple and painted one for himself to eat. After taking a bite he convinced me, there might be more to life than pulling weeds and tilling the earth until ones hands start to bleed. So I decided to take him up on his offer and we took a *Noonday Rest* under the shade of that tree.

While I laid there I fantasized of a life I could never afford tilling a dirty square plot of land. I dreamt of a field vast and wide and it was all mine, full of crops that were ready to be reaped for their rewards. I rode atop a gallant dark blue steed, pulling a plough through my dream like a rushing stream, racing towards the end in a hurry to leave the riverbed dry. Then I thought to myself why not a dozen horses, so that I would never have to do the work that had broken so many of our peoples backs over the years ever again.

They were wonderful dreams for any field hand to have and I went on and on about them. Botticelli had enough of my ramblings.

He threw his hands in the air and said, "Capture those dreams Fragonard, like you did the other night, the stars at your disposal for you to choose how you manipulate and play with them."

I didn't fully understand. I'd never taken the whole day off work and thought about it. He told me to look at my surroundings. This was my opportunity to escape from my reality, not expand upon it. To think outside of what the fields were to a farmer, but what they could be to a dreamer.

I thought to myself, I could have anything I want. It was a fairytale to manipulate how I choose. I searched for the abstract, an abnormality in the dull, placid landscape. Then I saw it, an object I could bend and mold to my imaginative will. The fields were like lumps of bobbing water in a swampy ocean of green hues and pleasant blues. The land filled with gigantic waves in a great flood, crashing against obstacles, changing course when they rolled over a hill or came into contact with a farm house. The crops then sprung to life and began swimming like minnows. The horses dropped to their bellies and set sail down the road into the wild blue yonder.

I'd finally created a dream like he did with the apple. The thrill I got from using my imagination was something I couldn't wait to experience again and again.

Then he picked up a rock and asked what I thought of it. To me it was just a plain ordinary thing to most, but then I closed my eyes and used my imagination. I dreamt of a pile of rocks as tall as a mountain, reaching the clouds in the sky and me standing on top as a master of the fields and my surroundings. He said it was a fair effort, but to keep working on my new skill later tonight when I had time for my dreams to easily come to life.

We returned home just as the sun was going down. My father was waiting for me, but with no supper at all. Apparently Grant Wood had seen us sleeping underneath that old tree and told my father about it. He was outraged and he had every right to be. There was no explaining my way out of this one. I'd wasted an entire day. I'll never forget what he said to me.

"You can spend the night outdoors sleeping under those stars you and your friend stare at every night. Tomorrow, if this daydreaming painter is gone and the chores are done, I'll think about letting you back in."

He then slammed the door behind him. I'd never seen him this upset. I didn't know what else to do. So I asked Botticelli if he could show him what I saw him do out in the fields with the apple.

Botticelli responded with his lips curled in a crooked uplifting manner, "Your father is not a daydreamer like us. Besides, he would never understand such a small feat of my ability's."

I thought perhaps he was right. My father would never believe in such foolish nonsense. So I told Botticelli to go out to the fields and sleep under the tree. In the morning, after he had a chance to cool down I would try to reason with him. He told me not to worry, he would find his own way to settle things with my father. I had no idea what he meant. I only hoped it wouldn't be the last conversation we shared. I did enjoy our talks on the way home from the fields.

The next day my father was up bright and early. He said he would be accompanying me to the fields. I asked if he was feeling up to the challenge.

My father griped back, "I wouldn't worry about me. Grant Wood will be giving us a lift. I'd be more concerned with yourself and the way you've been acting. There will be no sleeping on the job today."

I knew I was in trouble if Grant Wood was going to be there, I just hoped Botticelli had something up his sleeve that would save my reputation as well as his own.

We pulled alongside the road just as Botticelli was getting up from his nap. He was sleeping on a bed of odd looking flowers, ones I'd never seen grow in our fields. Grant Wood was in disbelief and so was my father. The land had been tilled and the crops were already planted. To be honest, I had no idea how he was able to put in so much work, even with the help of his brush.

My father thanked him for helping me with the chores. He then apologized and said he'd be able to return at night. In fact, he could sleep wherever he desire, so long as he was putting in an honest days effort. That's all my father really cared about. He wasn't concerned with what one did in their free time.

That evening we ate until our bellies were full. My father asked the typical questions throughout the meal. Where he came from, why he became a painter and what led to him ending up here in our neck of the woods. Botticelli replied the best he could with a mouthful of bread. His answers were vague. I don't think he wanted to talk about himself.

Botticelli put an elbow on the table and asked my father if he had any dreams. I thought he'd be put off by such a silly question, but he actually opened up. He said it'd be nice to live in a castle with a bell-tower and walls to protect us from the harsh winters. He talked about a courtyard with statues and fountains and beautifully trimmed hedges. He then looked at me and wished I didn't have to work so hard like he did when he was young.

After my father went to bed I asked Botticelli if we could use his brush to paint the stars like we did the other night. He said he had enough fun with his brush for awhile, then he handed me one of my own. I asked what magic this new brush could do. All he told me was the only magic it possessed was the ability to paint the things I saw around me on a canvas. It was a regular brush from his things. He said if I wanted to become a master like him, I might try spending our week off learning how to paint. I thought it was a splendid idea and a way for me to prove myself to him as a painter.

The next day I went out to the fields and spent an afternoon underneath the shade of that tree learning how to paint. The fields weren't much to look at and they never were. There was a lot of open space, farmyards and blue skies overhead. It all looked the same at first glance.

However, upon closer inspection I began to notice there were details in the landscape, a language to be spoken of its simplicity. The rocks and the rills weaving beyond the valleys, rolling over the templed hills, spanning widely across regiment fields. The silent miles of wind bent grasses, as she twists and turns throughout the sparse countryside. The shadows bouncing off the landscape, reflecting the changing moods of the sky. The outlines of trees ruffled in the backdrop and the secular rows of green and brown that careened down long winding alleyways cut deep into the earth.

There was an idea present in the dull placid atmosphere after all. The solitude, it was speaking to me in a way I never thought imaginable. Now all I had to do was find a way to convey this message on the canvas. So I rolled up my sleeves and then I got to work.

I felt for my first painting it should be indigenous to the soil, the culture in which I grew up in. I thought it should preserve our way of life in a narrative lending to the language of a farmer. I decided to keep things simple by using the texture and form of the geography, rather than relying solely on the subject matter to achieve my objective. For my palette I drew from the pigments of the earth to create something warm and inviting. I used a bright fauve to explain the fabric of the pastures and light greenish hues to exemplify the oval shapes of trees. Travertine colors like worn browns and creamy tans came in handy when I wanted to intensify where the land had eroded and become weathered.

Just as I was about to lay down the final strokes on some mulberry bushes, a nest of black birds jumped out of the fields in front of me. I immediately reacted, wanting to capture this moment as quickly as possible. So without thinking, I dipped my brush into a healthy swab of black and smeared them all over the canvas.

After the thrill subsided I stepped back from my work, amazed by what I could achieve, if allowed myself the chance to dream. You know, it wasn't until I captured the fields on the canvas that I realized how special and important they truly were to me.

By the end of that summer I had several paintings to show for my efforts. Mostly landscapes and farmyards, but occasionally I'd throw in something a little more showy like an interior. I still had a lot to learn about lighting and technique. The refinement of my palette needed some tweaking, but I was aware of it. Although I'll say this. I was well on my way to becoming a fine artist. One thing I excelled at was my own unique style and finesse. I was even able to write my own signature using just one single stroke.

Though our home was small, my father hung every painting I had. He invited the whole kingdom after Sunday brunch. I couldn't believe how many people showed. Landseer, Enstrom and his daughter Rhoda, Renoir and even Grant Wood made the long trip to town to see what all the fuss was about. I don't believe none of them had ever seen art like this hanging on a wall. It really brightened the room. Quite the contrast from the daily life. I was the talk of our community for many weeks afterwards.

Botticelli and I looked over my paintings before the people arrived. He wanted to give me an honest critique. He said my work was fair for a novice, but not yet that of a master. I better show improvement soon or I might find a new hobby, he scorned, one suited to my previous background.

I took his criticism well. However, over the past few centuries I've had the fortunate privilege to hang on the very same walls as my own artwork. I received an overwhelming amount of praise from fine-art connoisseurs and passer buyers contradicting his exact comments made long ago. One man even said I had the presence of Titian, the panache of Correggio and that my palette had the boldness and the flavor of Rembrandt. It was quite the complement.

Towards the end of the show I got up on a chair and started banging away on a glass with a fork to quiet the crowd down. Everyone gathered around the dinning room table and I announced a few gifts for some of my friends in the kingdom.

"To a good friend of many years. Enstrom, I present to you and your daughter Rhoda a painting simply called *Grace*. It is a gift for the bread you gave to us and our people many winters ago, as a token of my gratitude."

The crowd gave him a standing ovation. He said he would hang it in his bakery with honor and admire it for years to come. The painting was of a humbled man praying before his meal. It was fitting.

He and his daughter provided bread for the whole kingdom during a bad wintery season a few years back. He didn't ask for anything in return until next year's crops had been harvested. I never did truly thank him for his generosity. This new talent of mine allowed me the chance.

"Next I would like to present my father's old friend Grant Wood with a painting entitled, *Near Sundown*. It is my way of thanking you for being such a good neighbor and mentor over the years."

Grant Wood said the painting looked so real it was like a picture, plucked from the sunny voids of his fields. I didn't know what to say. This truly was a fruit of my new laborers I was glad to receive.

Then I presented Logan Landseer with his painting. I called it *The Shoeing of the Bay Mares*. It was my way of thanking him for keeping our horses trotting around on a pair of decent shoes. He said it was nothing, but I don't think our kingdom would manage so easily without him. He certainly was one of the hardest workers I have ever known.

I asked Renoir to stand up and take a bow next. Then I presented him with his gift, a piece I called *Lise Sewing*. It was a thank you for adorning our people over the years with their attire. I greatly admired the man. He truly was a symbol to all those who traveled to the kingdom of Fragonard looking for a fresh start. He had very humble beginnings as a pottery maker, a craft he learned back home. The work just wasn't cut out for him. Uneven bowls, wobbly plates, misshapen jars. Then one day he got the idea to pick up a needle and thread and he hasn't stopped sowing since. Enstrom couldn't have been happier that day.

My father asked if I had a painting to hang in our home. I said of course. I presented him with *Rinaldo in the Gardens of Armida*. It was a painting of a garden like the one he told me about in his dream, if we ever could afford to plant one so lavish. He smiled favorably and said he was glad to have a son to one day rule over his lands, whom thought of his father and his people so fondly.

Of course I couldn't forget Botticelli, who inspired me to paint these magnificent visions in the first place. So I presented him with his gift last but not least. I called the painting *A Summer Night*. It was what I thought the island he visited might look like. I didn't try to recreate this reality, I sought to give it the dreamlike quality it deserved. The legend of the mythical horse. The luminous fairytale butterflies, the surreal forest he wandered though and the bizarre creatures he described. He said it was my finest work as he marveled over the detail. I truly felt I'd found my niche and it was all thanks to this painter who mysteriously showed up in town one day.

After everyone left, my father patted me on the back and broke out his best bottle of green ale. We drank on through the night and for once, he actually forgot about the chores that needed to get done.

While we were sitting at the table, enjoying the left over crumbs from a loaf of Enstrom's bread, my father asked when Botticelli was going to get around to painting his portrait.

Botticelli replied, "In due time my King. I will paint you a work of art only a master can dream. Perhaps when the work in the fields is done."

On that note my father realized we still had a long day ahead of us in the morning. So he put his bottle of ale away and said goodnight.

VI

CRADLING WHEAT

"Stefan, Help! There's this dreadful little fly buzzing around my face, causing my nose to itch. If you wouldn't mind, could you brush it away and swat it for me? I would be forever grateful and in your debt."

"Where? I don't see anything. I think you're imagining things."

"Look, it just flew over there. Hurry, I can still hear its wings chattering about down the hallway like the loud thomping tail of the bitter north-easterly winds."

"Hold on, I'll get it."

Fragonard clinched his fist tight, "What a scoundrel the dirty little fly is. You would be my hero if you did."

Stefan picked up a newspaper someone left in the museum, rolled it up and swatted the fly in one gallant blow. He then presented it before Fragonard.

"Oh, EKK! Don't show it to me. Take it away at once."

Stefan shuffled the newspaper toward him and said, "Don't tell me you're scared of one little fly?"

Fragonard veered back, his nose in a twist, "No, it's just that. You try living in a painting. It's incredibly difficult to maintain oneself in this condition."

"I can't believe it would be that hard. You've got a light on all night and no one to bother you."

"You'd think it would be easy, but if it isn't something as simple as a fly, when the dust settles all seems to go wrong. Now please, remove this ghastly thing from my sight before I become ill."

"Okay, I'll throw it away."

Stefan threw the fly away and then he sat back down on the bench.

"So Stefan, earlier when we met you said you lost the inspiration to paint. I remember you saying something about how your father thinks it's a waste of time."

"He says I should grow up and put the brushes away, but all I've ever wanted to do since I can remember is paint and create art."

"You know I never had a chance to grow up, only to grow old. So why does he think choosing a path as an artist is childish?"

"I was told it's not a real profession. He says I'll end up penniless and living on the streets because I won't make any money doing what I love."

"You were told this? I've know a few artists throughout the years who would easily argue otherwise."

Stefan leaned forward and said, "Really, like who?"

"Take for instance the exclaimed painter, Jean François Millet."

"You knew him personally?"

"Well, no. Not personally. Although I do believe I met him in passing once as he was meandering his way though the halls of this museum. I'm sure if we had the chance to chat it would have been enlightening."

"So how did he become an artist?"

"He started out as a field hand on his father's farm. Hard work was something he knew well by the time he became of age. The skills he learned as a child lead to his path to becoming an artist. At the party I was attending some pretty big numbers were being tossed around for his works of art."

"It couldn't have been easy starting out as a farmer. I'll bet it took him forever to achieve his dreams."

"That painting you took down earlier. It's called *The Gleaners*, one of my favorite pieces by the man. It's sat across from me for years. The three woman are going through a field and picking up what's left after harvest. Their work has only just begun, but I bet they'll have that field cleared before you know it."

"How am I going to clear a field?"

"It's about the efforts you put forth, not the work that you do. You have to start somewhere. You very well can't get anywhere if you feel you are going nowhere. So what are you going to do?"

"I don't know yet. I want my father to be proud of me, but he's right. Being an artist isn't practical."

"So this is what's really bothering you. Practicality. You're worried you won't amount to anything like Thomas Hart Benton."

"Whose Thomas Hart Benton?"

"He was a regionalist who sought to bring to life the common man on the canvas. His father as well didn't see how being an artist was practical. Of course, he was a well to do aristocrat. I doubt he would have understood. Despite his struggles with his father, he went on to become one of the greatest muralists to ever live."

"That's them. I'm not anyone special and I haven't accomplished anything great."

"Our dreams are but a small, quiet breath of air had in our lives. Whispered once and then forgotten by the time we try to speak of them aloud. Another voice from another time. What I'm trying to say is you may have chosen a different path than your father's, but that doesn't mean it is of less value and not worth pursuing."

"I guess, I'll think it over."

"Good, you do that. I'll never forget Benton's painting, *Cradling Wheat*. What a wonderful achievement. Had he given up, the world would never know. There is however one thing I never understood about the piece that hung next to it.

What was that mechanical thing they kept stuffing full of crops?"

"Fragonard, I don't even know what to say about that."

"In the meantime, why don't you fetch another painting for me to view as I continue with my story."

"I could find a landscape or a portrait?"

"Not another portrait. Surprise me with something from the other room. I think that's where they keep the abstract art, though I can't be sure. Rarely do I get a chance to see what they have in there."

"Okay, I'll go see what I can find."

Stefan wandered into the other room. He looked over the paintings, searching for one he thought Fragonard would like. There was one that had an assortment of brightly dotted colors meticulously placed onto the canvas. He lifted it up and brought it back to him, then he leaned the painting against the wall.

Fragonard tried focusing in, "There's something wrong with this painting. It appears to be pixelated. Could you bring it a little closer?"

"Here Fragonard, let me wipe the dust off your eyes."

"Thank you. It's been awhile since I've had a good dusting."

Stefan lifted himself up on his toes and carefully wiped the dust over Fragonard's eyes with his sleeve. He then stepped back and said, "There, now have a look."

"What do we have here. The use of color is absolutely stunning. No, alarmingly beautiful. Such vibrancy and enriched tone. Who painted this? I must know."

"You've never heard of this artist. It's called *La Grande Jatte* by Georges Seurat."

"Oh, that's the painting they keep talking about. Now that I've had a chance to view it for myself personally, I must say it's not abstract at all."

"I'm glad you like it. So can I hear the rest of your story now?"

"Of course. Have a seat and I'll continue with my story, but before I do I'll leave you with a thought. My father used to say this to me all the time. You can work hard throughout the summer months tending to the fields and the chores, but if you don't harvest them at the end of the season, then you will starve in the winter. Trust me. I know."

Stefan sat back down on the bench with two fingers and a thumb pressed against the sides of his chin and continued to listen to his story.

"Where did I leave off? Oh yes, I remember now..."

VII

THE KING'S NEW CASTLE

Harvest season was finally upon us. It came around quicker than I thought that year. Botticelli wasn't looking forward to the work ahead and neither was I. I'd spent nearly the entire summer without doing a single chore. I couldn't wait to spend my day's indoors doing what I truly loved, painting to my heart's desire.

The night before harvest I woke Botticelli and asked if he was up to such a challenge. He said he already had a plan in mind, but that it would require his old attire and long billowy hat. I retrieved his old attire and when he put his hat back on, I knew he had something special planned.

So off we went for a stroll down the main road of town. When we passed by Landseer's Botticelli covered his mouth and coughed, "The air is wretched Fragonard, simply wretched. Is this anyway to live, in such filth?"

I said there was nothing I could do and that, that was the way our people had always lived.

He smiled in response with the crookedness seen on his lips as he often did and said, "Ah, but there is something I can do, if I were to receive a gracious gift from your father."

"And what would that be?" I asked with an insatiable smile.

"Why the title of Royal Painter of course."

If he really wanted this title to be bestowed upon him, I told if he removed the dirt in the roads and then painted a stroke of luck over the entire kingdom, he'd be praised by our people for years to come and receive his highly sought after position without question.

Botticelli smirked with enthusiasm, as he swiped his magic over the road, removing the dirt and debris. He then paved the streets in with the oils on his palette. Everywhere we walked that night, it was the first thing he did, as if a red carpet was being laid out to complete this dream of ours.

We'd been walking for so long, eventually we looped back around to my father's humble little home. There I watched as he painted us a sparkling white palace. The new castle had beveled crowns, turrets and archways. It was surrounded by curtained walls with gargoyles hanging over the edges. I know the crows certainly would think twice before nesting in them. Then I pointed over at the bell tower. With a gentle upward stroke, it grew like a giant bean stalk twisting into the air. I wondered though, how would anyone be able to hear it ringing in the morning from all the way up there?

To finish the job, he painted a grand row of trees on either side of the road leading up to the main entrance. They were quite beautiful, filled with plenty of his green, ambitious character. I thought the birds would enjoy them in the summer and the squirrels would particularly enjoy them in the winter.

Now that my father finally his dream come true, I asked what was next on the list for tonight's performance. Botticelli put a hand on his chin as he mused over this thought.

"You once mentioned how the courtyard was nothing more than a dirt road running through the center of town. What do you think we should do about this young Ayden, Prince and heir to a former pile of dirt?"

I knew exactly what I wanted, as I eagerly replied,

"I know, how about a lavish garden, a place of paradise for dreamers such as ourselves to sit and gaze upon the stars at night."

Botticelli's smile lifted along with mine. He told me to step back as he was about to unleash a true test of his skill. He raised his brush in the air, and crafted that dirty square plot of land into a monumental work of art. Paint was flying everywhere. We were lost in a forest of shrubs and perennials and winding pathways. The most beautiful flowers were scattered throughout. Every variety you could think of was blossoming before us as if spring had just arrived. I couldn't even begin to count the ways in which he'd easily painted them to life.

We took a stroll through the new garden so he could chisel out some statues. He talked about each one of these people he created, detailing their mannerisms, giving insight as to their contributions to his own artistic style. His boyhood friend Andrea Del Sarto, whom he often found copying his work. His rival Correggio and Fra Filippo, an old teacher of his who liked to ramble on about the golden rule, while he was asleep in a chair.

Now that the garden had been planted I mentioned, "You should paint your bed of grass and flowers, so that you'll have a place to sleep when the work is done."

Botticelli humbly replied, "I'll get to it later on Fragonard, after the chores have been taken care of, of course."

86

He was right. There was only so much of the night left before the early morning bell rang above my father's new home, revealing the magical surprise that awaited everyone. Landseer had a faulty gate that needed to be fixed. It seemed every other day one of his horses would get loose and trot off and wander through town. The sign above Enstrom's bakery certainly was in need of some new paint and Renoir had a leaky roof that could use some mending. I knew we couldn't walk around all night taking care of these tedious chores.

So Botticelli and I walked to the edge of town where I first met him. He swiped his brush over a pile of debris and rubble ready for the trash, transforming it into a mountain of enriched soil. It was tall enough to reach the peak of the shortest tower on my father's new castle and gave us a clear view of the whole kingdom. He painted it full of lush green grasses, each blade unique and colorful with its own whimsical charm.

There at the top I watched as he painted the rest of our kingdom from rags to riches. The homes magically grew in size and everyone had their own fenced in yard. After he cleaned up the rest of the streets, he painted a wall surrounding our village to protect us from the harsh winters.

Since most of the work was done, I asked if I could paint a few things. It'd been awhile since he let me play with the brush and I'd learned so much since the last I used it.

Botticelli yawned and said, "Maybe another night Fragonard. I'm awfully tired. For now, I think I shall create that bed of flowers you talked about. I am going to need a place to sleep tonight."

I was getting awfully tired myself. So we turned our attention to the fields. I could see Grant Wood's farmyard in the distance and my square plot of land off to the side. It looked so small from up there, I wondered how I ever made a living farming such a hovelled piece of land.

Botticelli instantly had his eye on that tree he was so fond of. He worked his magic and lifted it atop two hills he created out of thin air. Then he swiped his brush over the landscape, covering it in a pastelic dream, completely devoted to his strange and surreal flowers. Some patches grew in wild, running through it like an untamed river, whereas others were dictated by his palette, contained in rectangular blocks of color. It was a cluttered mess of beauty to revere and admire.

Though I thought it was all quite lovely, I pointed out how now neither Grant Wood nor I no longer had any crops to harvest. He said not to worry, he would make sure to paint a lavish feast for our people to enjoy every night and that no one in our kingdom would starve in the winter or go hungry ever again. I thanked him for his generosity and assured him, our kingdom would be forever indebted to him for his kindness.

The night of our dreams was fading and so Botticelli walked out to the two hills and fell asleep under the tree. I found a nice comfortable spot in the courtyard just outside the new castle. The next morning my father woke me up and asked if I knew what happened to his village while he slept. I told him everything about Botticelli and his magic brush. Pleased with all he had given us and the hard work he put in, we decided to let him sleep the day away for our gratitude.

Later in the evening Botticelli painted a lavish feast for everyone to enjoy as he had promised. After dinner, he was bestowed the title of Royal Painter and was allowed to sleep whenever, wherever he so desire from then on. The whole kingdom rejoiced at an end to their poverty, but what no one knew at the time is at what cost it would truly bring for our people.

When harvest season was over with we barely had enough crops to last us through the winter. It quickly became apparent as the last of the leaves began to fall, we'd have to rely solely on Botticelli's magic to sustain a living. In just that short amount of time my father had grown quite accustom to his newfound wealth and lifestyle.

Night after night he would meet up with Botticelli atop the bell-tower to discuss the layout of the town, deciding something as silly as the direction of a road. The next day he would change his mind and have him paint it all over again. I tried reasoning with him on more than one occasion, yet my father felt a man with such a talent would waste it, if he did not use it to its full potential.

Meanwhile the people were suffering from his lack of leadership. The larger the kingdom grew, the more there was to maintain. The paved roads started causing problems with drainage, something we'd never dealt with before. The price of a loaf of bread went up three-fold at Enstrom's bakery, what with people conserving what little they had. It seemed for every one thing we gained to make our lives easier there was always another problem that had to be dealt with. My father treated these issues as if though they were secondary to his living.

It all kept mounting, until one evening the people finally had enough. They were piled outside the main hall, demanding food and other provisions as well. My father was sitting down to another lavish meal perfectly painted on top of the table. I feared what would happen, if he didn't handle some of the larger issues. Food was becoming scarce and here we were looking like a gooses rear smothered in honey.

Grant Wood entered the room with a fist full of lilacs and daises in his hands.

He plainly spoke, "My fields have been turned into a grove of flowers. What will I eat throughout the winter months? You can't eat the daises."

My father, with a jolly smile filling his cheeks, lifted a goblet made of solid gold and replied, "Your fields, you old grouch. They might as well be a gift to Botticelli for the many things he has provided for us. So if you have too, yes, eat the daises and be thankful for them."

Grant Wood left shaking his head at the way he was treated by his dear old friend.

My father then asked if there were anymore servants of the kingdom outside his door to deal with before he sat down to eat. Enstrom entered the room, complaining about the last meal provided for the people. Botticelli had turned the sides of a green apple into but a mere baker's dozen. He was so busy with my father's demands, he hadn't found the time to produce any other means of sustenance.

"My daughter and I can't make a living dividing apples up into slices. Perhaps you could see it in your heart to give us more than a handful of crumbs?"

My father pounded his fist on the table, "I've been more than generous with you and your daughter. Be grateful for what you have and learn to make apple pie with it."

He then took a hearty bite off a chicken leg and ordered him away and ordered no more complaints be brought to his table for the rest of the evening. He didn't want the painter's talents wasted on what he felt were foolish requests with no merit.

My father then started to make foolish requests of his own, as if Botticelli were his own personal servant.

"Painter, would you please pass the sugar and if you wouldn't mind, I have spilt some gravy on my new robe."

Botticelli took out his brush, wiped the stain from his robe and then he swiped it over the sugar bowl. Just as the stain on my father's robe was no more, the sugar bowl promptly sprouted legs and walked down the table passed twenty-nine empty chairs. It was a true show of my father's absolute arrogance. He then started in on my appearance, though it had never been a problem before.

He looked at my attire and then his own with a sneering glare, "Painter, my son is still wearing the clothes of a field hand. Paint him a new robe, one fitting for a Prince. While you're at it, paint one for me as well, one made of fine linen with gold and silver thread."

After those ridiculous orders were made I knew my father had truly become the essence of a lazy oaf. No longer a servant of the people, but a servant to his new tastes in life.

When the table was cleared and Botticelli left the room, I tried to get in a word on the way he'd been acting. Though I found it difficult, what with him rambling on about his newfound wealth and how he should spend it.

"Son, you know that garden you keep. It's an overgrown mess. We should have Botticelli paint it away next spring and put in a ballroom. Yes, a ballroom. So we'll have a place to throw lavish parties. What do you think?"

"I think you're treating the people unfairly."

"What do you mean? I treat the people just fine. Now what about this ballroom. Should we have inlaid floors or heaping slabs of green marble?"

"I'd like to talk about Grant Wood. You've known him for years and yet tonight..."

"Oh that ornery old goose. He'll get over it. He has a way of making due with what he has. Now you were saying marble would look better. I have to agree."

"Are you listening to me at all? For every order you give, that's a loaf of bread off of someone's table."

"All this talk about who has what and who does not. I find it boring. Let's talk about my ballroom. Besides, we can have anything we want. Just ask your friend. He doesn't mind, and you shall receive. In fact, that should be our new motto."

"Our new motto? This is absurd. We should think of the wellbeing of the people, not what type of flooring you want in your ballroom."

"Son, you don't understand. No longer do I have to handle the affairs of land disputes and the prices of crops in the fall. Servants work. It's time I lived like a real king and you started acting like a real prince. Now about this ballroom."

While my father continued to talk about flooring, I went out to the courtyard and sat down on a bench to think things over. Botticelli was there painting up some wheat and barley for Grant Wood.

There were a long line of people waiting behind him, asking for help to get them through the coming winter months ahead. I was grateful someone hadn't forgotten what made our kingdom so special.

After Botticelli painted the last loaf of bread, he sat down next to my side and said.

"I've see this type of behavior before. All too often in the places I've visited, where the wealthy lived in ivory towers, quite literally. While the people they were supposed to be watching over lived in squalor beneath those thrones of high society."

It was a shame, he told me, but it was my father's choice to bear this burden and he grudgingly chose to bare it alone. I agreed, the man I once admired was no longer my father, but a spoiled rotten child. Botticelli said, if it would make me happy he'd stop painting the lavish things my father kept demanding. He promised from now on no more robes of fine linen, towers adorned with gold and silver, jewel encrusted crowns and food for plenty at an empty table.

The next night my father sat at his throne and started making his foolish demands. It was a laundry list of luxury a mile long. He asked for a grander dinning hall, embroidered carpets, softer shoes, a larger bed and more towers, one standing taller than the next.

Botticelli stood up, stretched his arms and yawned. He then announced he was tired. He said the King would have to wait for his riches another day. My father stood up and asked he paint himself a throne by his side.

Botticelli humbly replied, "Ah, but where will your son sit, if not by your side?"

My father, after hearing those words realized he'd made a grave mistake. He promised from now on he would not think of himself, but of the good of the people and his son. He then looked at me for forgiveness, as he pulled out a chair and asked if I would sit by his side. Botticelli smiled favorably with his lips arguably sealed in a crooked manner.

Later in the evening I met up with Botticelli to thank him personally for bringing my father back to his senses. He was gazing upon the stars as he often did, watching over them as if they were flowers in his own personal garden.

He asked if I would still love my father and stand by his side, even if he couldn't learn from the error of his ways. Of course I would, that was an easy question to answer. He reminded me that my father would never understand dreamers such ourselves. He was right, I'll admit that. My father's dreams, though were met with good intent before he had his wealth, weren't anything like what Botticelli and I dreamed of.

He then spoke of his own father. It was the first time I ever heard him speak of the man.

"My father was just like yours in many ways. When he acquired everything he ever wanted, he forgot he even had a son. I'm afraid your father will one day do the same to you."

I replied, "I hope that day never arrives. I would be lost without him."

He put a hand on my shoulder and pointed to the heavens. "That star, the one right over there. It is known as the dreamers star. If you ever do feel lost, follow that star Fragonard. It will guide you down the right path."

Botticelli asked how I was coming along with my new talents. I told him I painted every day and adhered to his advice closely. He smiled, pleased that I was following in his footsteps. I asked if we could share in another night of magic and staring up at the stars in the sky. He thought perhaps we could share a night around the courtyard, painting with regular brushes instead. I thought it was a nice gesture and so we spent the rest of the evening painting the thoughts in our heads.

VIII

FRAGONARD'S DREAM

In the Garden of Rococo

The months quickly passed us by. Winter was now a daily chore for our people to contend with. The windows were covered in frost and the streets were a mess of ice and sleet. Renoir could barely keep up with the demand for overcoats and hats. Enstrom and his daughter had their work cut out for them serving up warm bowls of soup to keep everyone fed. I remember Grant Wood came into town one day, struggling to pull his horse and cart through the piling drifts of snow. Landseer offered to lend him a helping hand, but he wouldn't have it. He was as stubborn an ornery as that old horse of his.

Botticelli had become a recluse, as the weather had withered away his bed of grass and flowers to nothing more than an icy chill, to cold to sleep on. He would wake every night and stand atop the bell tower. There he would stay until morning, tirelessly gazing out into his once glorious field of strange and surreal flowers. Try as he may to rid himself of this problem, his magic wasn't powerful enough to combat against the determined forces of nature. It seemed he would just have to wait until spring for everything to melt before he could enjoy his garden of paradise, reminiscent of his dream.

By midwinter the artic winds started to settle in across the fields, bringing with a white haze of dense flurries that blanked the landscape. You could barely see the two hills poking out of the distance in this frozen wasteland. I tried cheering him up with a few paintings to remind him of the summer months and the coming spring ahead. He continued to pine as he toiled over the impossible, unable to accept defeat.

Then one night, during a terrible blizzard an idea spontaneously came to him in his dreams. He simply made the castle walls taller and curved to carry the prevailing winds elsewhere. Then he pulled a star from the nighttime sky, placed it above the bell tower and was able to keep his flowers in bloom. It created this magical bubble of warmth, stretching all the way to Grant Wood's farm. The people graciously applauded him. It was a much desired summer dream had by all.

I spent most of my days painting and hanging my artwork up around the castle. Throughout that time I longed to use his brush to create something magical of my own, but he was always too busy with some menial task brought on by my father or one of the villagers.

So one evening during a full moon I went looking for him, to see if perhaps we could paint the stars like we once did before. I'd learned so much since the last time we played with them, I was hoping to get a chance to show him how much I'd improved.

To be honest, I was growing bored with the usual things I painted. The spark of inspiration had withered and the fields had lost their luster on the canvas. I longed for change, desiring a real challenge I could tackle and master. It was then when I finally understood why he stared at the stars every night. He was searching for a new dream, an unreachable paradise hidden amongst the heavens somewhere.

I went out to the fields and found him asleep atop the two hills under the shade of that tree he was so fond of. The brush was already in his hand, as if he planned on staying awake to paint another masterpiece of his choosing. I didn't want to disturb him and besides, his dream had already come to fruition and mine was still waiting to be crafted. So I carefully removed the brush from his grasp, assuming he wouldn't mind if a likeminded master borrowed it for a little while. I then snuck away into the courtyard with a painter's palette of my own.

There in the courtyard I thought of all the wonderful things I could create with this dry and withered canvas of autumn before me. One thing for certain, the hedges were in need of a good pruning or we'd be fighting them back when summer rolled around. Some of them were so out of shape they resembled something closer to a furry beast rather then a work of art.

So I began hacking away, taming this hairy animal that needed to be properly groomed. I trimmed and pruned spires of blue rhombuses, sliced and diced cinnamon sticks out of the rosebushes and ginger bread loaves out of the hedges. I found the more I created, the bolder I became. Neapolitan evergreens, lemon drop ash trees and a bordello of licorice twists hanging in the willows.

The garden was cleaning up nicely when I noticed some vines strangling the life out of a box shaped Buxus. It looked completely entangled, snarled by its own tail. I just couldn't allow a blemished spot to tarnish my masterpiece in the making. So I unwound this leafy ball of green thread and coiled it around a trellis set against the bell tower. Then I thought, what else could I breathe new life into?

The flowerbeds were hibernating from the cold winter frost. I could easily handle this with a few simple strokes, but I was desiring more, a real challenge I could sink my teeth into. Then I remembered the night Botticelli had on the island and all those beautiful flowers he'd told me about that had broken free from their stems. I wondered if this might be a way for me practice, until I unlocked more of the secrets behind the magic of his brush.

I smeared some yellow paint on a wilted dandelion. Then, I curiously tickled gently under the lip of its chin to see if I could get it to wake up. The dandelion let out a loud yellow "ROARRRR" as it fluttered its pedals to life and flew away. I was ecstatic. It actually worked. I swabbed some lavender on a tulip and waited to see what would happen. It slowly opened its pedals and yawned. Then it hopped off its stem and started buzzing about like a humming bird. I tried this magic on an orchid next. To my amazement, it lifted off its stem and glided away like a ballerina dancing for my amusement.

I was having so much fun I decided to paint all the flowers in bloom, releasing them from their nocturnal slumber. The air was illuminated with sugar plum lilies, streams of yellow magnolias, ribbons of midnight blue pansies and twinkling aloft with periwinkle carnations. They swayed, waltzing in

ornamental arrangement under the direction of my
magic wand of sorts.

My dreams truly came to life in a way I never
thought imaginable. I had crafted a masterwork of art
on a living, breathing canvas. It was as if a fairytale
had come to life out of the pages of a book. Satisfied
with my efforts, I found a nice comfortable spot on a
bed of nesting lilacs and lay down. Soon thereafter I
fell asleep to buttercups, bluebells and zinnias zigging
and zagging out of my sights. It was absolutely
marvelous. You should have been there.

Hours later I woke in a chamber of greenery,
trapped in a forest barberry, boxwood and arctotis. I
had unknowingly unleashed a spell with the magic of
the brush, placing an enchantment of mammoth
proportions over the entire garden. The flora and
fauna must have been bathing in the fountains while
I slept, slurping up this enchanted oily brew until
there was nothing left.

I took the sharp end of my brush and carved
out an opening in this wall of green to see how bad
things had gotten. On the other side I discovered a
dense jungle of exotic colors and leafy green oddities.
There was no real path to follow, only the flowers
fluttering freely about in a chaotic haze of sparkling
dust drifting by in the air.

I knew I had to paint it away before sunrise or I would be in a lot of trouble with Botticelli and even more so with my father.

I could hear him speak to me in the back of my mind, "You should have been tending to the chores my son, instead of resting on the job."

His robust voice, the disapproval in his tone. I knew he was right, I should have been more responsible with my actions, but pining over it wasn't going to solve anything. There was only one way to win this fight, plain old hard backbreaking labor and a gallant effort to stick with it.

With no time to waste I traversed my way through this labyrinth of no good shrubbery. I got right into it. Swashing and slashing, I fought back a thorn bush, jousted with a juniper, maimed a marigold and I had a chat with a statue of a deep thinking thinker. I believe his name was Thomas Eakins. He rambled excessively about theory of concept or concept of theory as he walked in circles on a roundabout. I'm not really sure where he was going with any of it, although the plants seemed to enjoy his lofty banter.

Try as I may, my efforts to maintain a garden were to of no avail. I kept lapping on stroke after stroke, but the oils on my palette only seemed to be fueling this leafy mess, causing everything to thrive and flourish.

The pathways I'd already cleared out grew back in twice as thick and the hedges were as plump as an apple. The flowers I'd so easily brought to life acted more like mosquitoes, things to swat and shoo away. I was constantly nipped by tulips and orange blossoms. The snapdragons were the worst of it. Such a nuisance, little fiery beasts with wings. I plucked them pedal by pedal, but still they kept coming back for more.

I cut back a thicket of purple prickly pear and wandered into a tunnel made by the overhanging trees. It led me into a different part of the garden, one I don't remember Botticelli or I creating. The topiary was beyond surreal, an amusement park of abstract sculptures and obscure shapes. It had a dream like quality, magnificently bizarre, almost haunting in an artificial way. There were trapezoids and spherical objects set on pedestals. Hanging whirly dazzlers and succulents feasting on the flowers that would land down and take a drink of their sweet, yet deadly nectar.

The hedgerows had giant oval swoops carved into them. They were artistically crafted with arcs inclined at odd angles and uneven stripes graffitied into their foliage. It created these magical portals peering into an exhibit of weird and exotic plants. I saw a green hand reaching out of the ground grasping at the moon, its fingertips almost grazing the edge. There was a one-eyed peacock waving its colorful plumage. This bulbus, misshapen yew was stooped over, happily chomping on some honeysuckle, while a hedgehog played possum nearby.

The artistry was exquisite, far beyond my capabilities. There was no possible way I could have created this in a night, but I wondered who could have done this while I was asleep dreaming of all those beautiful flowers? I sat down on a bench with my head in my hand. There had to be a way to put everything back to normal, but how do you combat against something this cunning and invasive. I just needed to think outside of the box of flora and fauna I had contained myself in.

While I was musing over the daffodils gliding in the air, the conifers began squawking and ruffling their foliage. I got up and looked on ahead to see what had spooked them. The hydrangea cackled like a hyena and a whole nest of conifers spread their wings and flew away. Staring straight at me was a mean and nasty hornbeam. It huffed and puffed, stomping its hooves. The beast let out a primal roar. It then broke free from its roots and charged, thrashing everything in its path.

The garden sculptures got down from their pedestals and began acting like wild animals that had just been released from the zoo. I raised the brush in the air, ready to strike this armada of leafy green carnivores when a clematis crept up and coiled around my legs. They knocked the palette out of my hand, reached out and took the brush from my grasp. I was pulled to the ground and woven into a bushy trap. I kept twisting and turning, but my attempts to break free only made the vines grow tighter.

With a bit of hourglass thinking, I rolled over my palette, covering myself in splotches of paint. The flowers swooped down in large swarms, nipping and pinching, feasting on the oils until their bellies were full. They cut through just enough of the vines for me to wiggle free. Unfortunately, however, by then the brush was nowhere to be found.

Then it occurred to me. Of course, I should have known all along. I looked up the bell tower. Those slimy green snakes were spiraling toward the top with it, seeking the warmth from the star Botticelli placed there to keep this garden of paradise from frosting over. I couldn't be outdone by a common garden pest. What would I tell Grant Wood? He certainly would shake his head at this one, if he ever found out.

So I began climbing to the top, fighting tulips and daises along the way, knowing full well if I couldn't end it here then the world would be next. Or at the very least, I'd be grounded for a month and a half.

With one foot leaned in and a hand barely holding onto the trellis, I reached out to tug on the brush. The vines latched onto my arm and we began wrestling back and fourth for control. I tried forcing the tip against the winding of its throat. Then I swung at it again, striking with some gusto and a thick layer of impasto. In response, it grew back three more vile snakes at the head of this hissing monstrosity.

The slimy green tentacle then yanked the brush right from my grasp. I lost my footing and fell from the bell tower, landing softly on a thorn bush. I noticed something while I was brushing myself off. Concealed by a box shaped hedge was the core root of all of this. I ripped out a knotted mess of weeds, crawled under the hedge and then I rolled up my sleeves and pulled with all my might, until finally I'd untangled this *Garden of Armida* that had strangled my dreams all night long.

The vines quickly withered and died. It was a cruel thought, but hopefully they would spring back in the summer and live again, though maintained by a sharped pruners knife.

109

With the vines defeated, the flowers landed back on their stems and went to sleep. I corralled the flamingoes and the hippos and giraffes and the other wild things I'd unleashed back to their respective boundaries in the garden. Now all I had to do was restore the courtyard before the early morning bell rang.

Everything was dripping wet, saturated in an oily mess. It was far beyond repair, so I wiped myself a clean slate. Then I softened my palette with flushes of silky pearls, creamy hues and pastelic mauves. I used rosy shades as to make things jocular and fluid. Rather then leaving it a chaotic mess for me to clean up later on, I chose a graceful approach this time, decorating with ornate motifs and garnishing them with juicy pinks and minty greens. I used simplistic highlights and red chalky lines to lighten the mood, giving things a rustic quality more pleasurable to the eye. I made sure the strokes were broad and clear, loose yet vigorous with a lucid paleness, allowing for a more passionate composition to show. I then blurred out any rough edges by using a robust color scheme in the foreground and dark silhouetting outlines in the background.

When I was done with the restoration the artist in me was dying to leave behind a signature on my work. Most of the statues had already been repaired or replaced, all but two that had their faces removed. Lavina and Scultori, two sisters I knew from when I was very young. I thought why not? They should dawn the faces of these two marbled beauties. I hope they wouldn't mind if I borrowed them for my muse. I hadn't seen them since they moved to the countryside on the other side of town.

Now that the task of hard labor was through I rushed off to where Botticelli still lie asleep on his bed of flowers atop the two hills and just before sunrise, I put the brush back in his hand, vowing to never mess with the painter's magic ever again without his consent.

IX

THE KING'S PORTRAIT

Months had passed since I first played with the brush. My father was quite happy, as he had survived the whole winter without so much as a cold. Then one day early in spring he took on a terrible fever. I remember that time very well. I was taking a stroll with Botticelli through a new hallway added to the castle to display the paintings I had dreamt of over the winter. I was showing him the ones in particular I created to remember that night I borrowed his brush and tried painting my dreams into a reality.

The first painting I showed him was *The Path Intersect the Garden*, my failed attempts at maintaining a flowerbed. He asked why I painted such an entangled mess overgrown with weeds. I said it was a recreation of a dream or rather a nightmare I had after I ate some bad fruit before going to bed.

He said often times our greatest accomplishments come from our deepest fears, especially when one tries to understand them in an abstract manner.

Then I showed him *Rinaldo in the Enchanted Forest,* a scene from a fairytale my father used to read to me when I was very young. Well, that's what I told him and I suppose there was a partial truth to it. In actuality it was a painting meant to display when I finally pulled that last weed in the courtyard. It was by sheer luck I happened to stumble upon the root of the problem. One thing I learned from that night, you're not a man until you've wrestled with a fourteen-foot tall rhododendron.

The next piece was simply called *February.* He really took special note and marked on how the horse in the painting looked familiar to him. I explained it was what I thought the one he saw on the island might look like. He said it bore poor resemblance, but that it did strangely look like a horse he'd seen in a reoccurring dream over the winter. I laughed and told him we were truly kindred spirits, because it seemed we shared the same dreams at night. He agreed and then we continued to look at more paintings.

While I was showing him the next piece, discussing the finer points and overall composition I'd chosen to go with, Grant Wood stepped into the room and told me I better go to my father's chambers. He said he was feeling quite ill and was unable to get out of bed. I dropped everything and immediately rushed to his side. It was worse then I could've ever imagined. His face was pale, his forehead was burning up and he had a persistent cough. It hadn't been since last summer when I'd seen him this depraved and out of breath.

I asked if there was anything I could do. He said not to worry, he'd been through this before and he was sure he'd be fine after a good nights rest. I returned a little while later with a painting called *January* to help cheer him up. I hung it on the wall next to his bedside as a reminder of what our kingdom once looked like in the winter, before Botticelli freed us from the icy winds and the torrential downfalls of snow. He said it was my finest work. It proved my worth to him not only as a painter, but more importantly as a son who stuck with it and succeeded beyond his wildest expectations.

By the end of the week my father took a turn for the worse. It seemed he might not last more than a few days at best. I cried many tears by his bedside and prayed continuously throughout the night he would show a sign of recovery, but by the next day it was obvious he wasn't getting any better. He was always good to me. He taught me everything I know young Stefan, so anything I could have sacrificed would have been an easy thought.

I went for a stroll around the courtyard to deal with this troubling un-expected turn in his health. Grant Wood was consoling me for my grief, when a foolish thought entered my mind. The brush, it could do almost anything. The possibilities were endless, limited only by ones imagination. I'd moved stars, created a lavish garden of paradise and built an entire kingdom with a single stroke of luck from that brush. It had to work, it just had too.

I went out to the fields to ask him if this dream of mine were possible. I remember the grass around the two hills had grown in unusually wild and untamed, tailored to Botticelli's eccentric lifestyle. There was a double rainbow that was beginning to fade in a dizzy haze over the flowers he had begun to paint the night before.

There he was on top of his mountain of grass and flowers, taking a nap under the shade of that tree he was so fond of.

I shrugged him on the shoulders, pleading with desperate emotions, "Botticelli, please wake up. There isn't enough time, you must come with me at once."

He slowly got up from his nap as his eyes resisted the urge to close, "Why have you disturbed me so early in the day? Isn't there some chores that must be taken care of?"

"My father, he is on his deathbed as we speak. If your brush is truly magical, than I was wondering if you could save his life with it."

He rubbed his eyes clean and replied, "Is this what's bothering you? I've never performed such a spell with the brush. I'm not even sure if it would work. There could be consequences, far beyond my understanding."

"I realize this, but if we don't do something now, surly he will pass."

Botticelli put a hand on his chin as he thought it over,

"Alright Fragonard. I'll see what I can conjure up, but in order for a dream as grand as this to come to fruition, I'll need all the sleep I can get so that my mind can wander and dream of such a spell."

I asked how much sleep he would need to dream this dream of dreams impossible to most, but certainly not for the painter. He said we'll just have to wait and see. I thanked him and told him if there was anything I could do, don't hesitate to ask and he would receive. He said in fact there was as he propped his back up against the tree with a big smirking, crooked grin.

"Oh there is one thing you could do for me. Round up all the paint in the kingdom, every last drop that you can find. If I do conjure up such a dream, I will need every shade at my disposal."

"I promise, on my word as a Prince, you'll have every last drop of paint in this kingdom by nightfall."

He then pulled his hat down and in a snide manner said, "Now I'm awfully tired. Please, leave me alone so I can finish with my dream."

I thanked him again for offering his magic and then I visited with my father to tell him the good news. Though I should have paid closer attention to Botticelli's callous behavior.

My father's complexion was supremely dark. The fever had taken even more out of him. I told him Botticelli was dreaming of a cure as we spoke. He said not to worry. All that mattered is that if he should pass, he was glad to know I would inherit a kingdom of wealth, no longer in poverty and that he knew he'd raised a son whom would be good to the people.

He then asked the one question any son fears a father will ask when lying on their deathbed. He wanted to know if he was a good father who had been good to his son throughout his life. Of course I said yes. That was an easy question to answer. My father tried to speak again. I told him to rest, he'd need it. Then I reassured him Botticelli would find a way to cure him. Though secretly, deep down inside I questioned if that were even true for someone as talented as him.

The next night I was called to my father's bedside. He was on his last few breaths, as all the kingdoms paint lay before him at Botticelli's request. I held his frail hand and he smiled back. I could tell he was at peace, knowing his son and closest friends were by his side. I called for Botticelli to be brought to my father's chambers. His fate was left up to his dream and my worst nightmare. Word came back that he was in such a deep slumber no one could break its spell. No matter, at least I knew he tried, the only way he knew how.

I was sure the light in his eyes would fade, when my father's chamber doors swung open. Botticelli, the painter walked in with brush in hand, an easel under his arm and a rather small canvas. He had an exited look in his eyes. He told us not to worry. He had a grand vision while asleep on his bed of flowers.

I cleaned my face of tears, wide eyed and hopeful, then I asked about this dream he conjured up. First, he said everyone but me must leave the room and if we valued his life, we'd act at once and do exactly as he asks. Grant Wood was the last one out the door. He left shaking his head, unsure to trust this man that had turned his fields into a grove of useless flowers.

Botticelli locked the door and then he told us of his dream. He said in order to save my father he would have to paint his portrait by painting him onto the canvas. This wouldn't cure him, but it would prolong his life, until he could think of the exact mixture to paint him back to health. The idea seemed a bit farfetched, but at the time I felt there was no other choice. So I nodded in agreement for Botticelli to commence with his plan.

Botticelli nodded back and then he set the easel down next to my father's bedside and carefully placed the canvas on it. He then dipped the brush into some white paint, the shade of the canvas and swiped it across his blank slate. The canvas grew in size, until there was enough room for my father's entire stance. I watched as he mixed together color after color with madness in his eyes, until finally he had what he needed laid out on his palette. He then set up the rest of his things and got to work. Swipe after swipe, my father slowly appeared before me on the canvas.

When Botticelli was done applying the last stroke he stepped back, admiring his handy work. I was mesmerized by this spell he placed over him as well. It was all so unbelievably strange. He could speak and move freely, just as I speak to you now young Stefan.

Every single wrinkle on his face was completely visible. His eyes, they beveled in a glossy sheen. The colors of his clothes and the way his ruby red robe swayed. It was as if he'd blended reality with the oils on his palette, producing perhaps his finest work.

My father had this distinguished look of pride, though I knew this isn't what he wanted, I assumed it would only be temporary. I'll never forget my father's voice. The words he spoke to me, it sounded like an enchanting echo ringing through the thick veneer of paint.

"My son and only heir, the task of taking care of the kingdom is in your hands now. Rule wisely over the people. Do not squander the power as I have over these past few months, but with the principles this kingdom was founded on, the ones that I have instilled in you over the years."

I promised him I would abide by his wishes on my word as a humble servant of the people, until he was painted out of the canvas and in good health.

I then met up with Botticelli a top the bell-tower to discuss what he would need to do next. He was crafting the stars, orchestrating something grand and magnificent. I could tell, the way his crooked smile lifted and the way his eyes sparkled as he played with the dreamy essence of the cosmos. It was quite haunting.

"It's an awfully quiet night Fragonard. You can hear the wind creating a dream of its own. Isn't it beautiful?"

"It is, I suppose in its own majestic way."

"Yes, it is. To me. Tell me, do you have a dream of your own? I mean one that isn't your fathers?"

"I would like to have a dream of my own, someday. All I really care about right now is my father's health. Why do you ask?"

"What if your father doesn't pull through? If I can't save his life, then... He did leave you in charge of the kingdom."

"If he doesn't pull through I'll be left with a lot on my plate. There will no longer be time for such foolish things as dreams when there's work to be done."

"Work? Think of it Fragonard, a dream beyond all we know as reality, free from the trappings of society where artists such as ourselves can do whatever we please without worry. Your father would never understand such a dream. He would squander it, but you and I."

"It would be a wonderful dream. I don't doubt it, but without my father it wouldn't be a dream worth having.

Botticelli left it at that. I could tell he wasn't happy with my reply, but my mind was somewhere else as you can imagine.

The next night I waited patiently as Botticelli struggled into the wee hours trying to blend together a palpable hue to my father's likeness. By midnight Botticelli threw his palette down. He didn't have to say a word. He was exhausted, pushed beyond the brink of his capabilities. Perhaps this was his dream, the one he could not obtain that lay beyond the stars. Well, it certainly was mine.

I told him it would be alright if he took a break. He earned it, besides my father was safe for now, as far as I knew.

He asked to be left alone with a week of no disturbances to help keep his mind clear and allow for his dream to fully come to fruition. He painted a door on my father's wall, next to his bedside. He opened it up and asked if I would help him with another task. I moved the paint inside the closet, so the secret to his wellbeing would be safe and secure.

Once again I did all the work while Botticelli sat back and watched, but I was glad to know it was for a good cause. After the paint was secured in this mystical closet of sorts, he shut the door and painted a magical lock over it, his brush being the key. My father's fate was now in the hands of a true masterful painter.

X

The Madness of King Fragonard

At the end of the week I checked in on my father to see if Botticelli had any luck painting him back to health.

To my udder joy, before I could even make it down the hallway he opened his chamber doors. I rushed to his side and he razzed my hair. He said he'd never felt better. His cheeks were full of color and merriment and best of all he no longer had a persistent cough. I couldn't believe it. Botticelli's magic had not only saved him, but reinvigorated him as well.

Unfortunately our celebrations were cut short. My father had some terrible news. Botticelli slowly began to suffer from the same illness as him and had to paint himself onto the canvas. It was a shame, he worked so hard to save my father's life. I asked to speak with him, to at least thank him for all that he'd sacrificed, but my father wouldn't allow it. He feared I'd catch the same horrible illness and I too would have to be painted onto a canvas.

I asked if there was anything I could do. I felt
I owed my life to him. He said in fact there was.
Botticelli proclaimed I was the only one with the skill
and the talent who could paint him back to health,
but that first I had to prove my worth to him as a
painter and a daydreamer. Then and only then
would I be allowed to see my friend.

Over the next few weeks I spent every waking
hour honing in on my craft. I'd take my work to my
father and he would show it to Botticelli for his
critique. I never received any praise or gratitude for
my efforts. He would just point out the faults and the
flaws, denoting the line-work and the use of color in
my palette. I was told it was too flowery for his tastes,
lending toward the abstract. That he needed absolute
realism and nothing less would suffice. Try as I may,
there was no pleasing him and to be honest I didn't
feel I could produce the art he wanted anyways.

One night after dinner in the main hall he
reviewed the best of my paintings. I remember we
were looking over a piece entitled, *The Bolt* and it
clearly didn't appease his tastes.

He stood in front of the painting and said,
"You call this art? It's awful. You'll never achieve
greatness at this rate. I might as well send you back
out to the fields and have you stick with what you're
really good at."

"I'm trying father, but it's difficult when I don't even know what he wants from me."

My father rubbed his hand on his chin and said, "Son, all is relying on you. You've shown improvement lately, but you could do better."

I asked again to speak with Botticelli to try and get some direction. My father said his illness was still highly contagious. It took the best out of him and he couldn't imagine what it would do to me.

"You're just going to have to double your efforts. If you don't, he'll become nothing more than a memory fading with the sun on a wall in this castle."

"It's just that I can't concentrate anymore. It's becoming difficult to even pick up a brush."

I was in shock by his response. I'd never seen him lose his temper so abruptly. He slammed his fist down on the table as hard as he could and erupted at me with great passion.

"So this is how you repay a debt of gratitude. I will not tolerate a son who does not abide by my wishes. From now on you'll have to spend your nights outdoors sleeping on Botticelli's bed of dreams. Maybe, after a few nights spent under the stars you'll find that spark on inspiration to appease me."

He then grabbed me by the collar and promptly escorted me to the gates and told me not to come back, until I choose to live under his thumb.

Over the next few weeks I slept under the shade of the tree atop the two hills where Botticelli used to dream. I would wake up bright and early and look out into the empty voids of the fields until the sun went down. I stared at the stars every night waiting for inspiration to strike, but it just wasn't happening. Whether Botticelli was ill or not, laying about staring at the same stars every night wasn't going to solve anything.

I stopped by Grant Wood's before going on the long walk home. I was hoping he could offer me some advice on the matter. I arrived just as he was packing the last of his belongings on a cart. I asked if he was planning on taking a trip. It appeared as if he wouldn't be returning anytime soon. He thought I already knew. My father showed up early in the morning, before sunrise and told him to pack up his things and leave. His farm was to be turned over by the end of the day, so his land could be presented to Botticelli as a gift for saving my father's life. I thought this just couldn't be. I promised I would talk with my father and sort this out, but he wouldn't have it.

The last thing Grant Wood told me I'll never forget. He said I was a hard worker, not to ever lose that side of me and to always remember my father, the way he once was. He then pulled on the reins of his horse and rode away shaking his head. I couldn't believe he was leaving nor that my father would treat him so poorly. With him gone, I knew something just wasn't right.

On the walk through the countryside I noticed the weeds had grown in thick. No one was left to tend to them anymore. Where had they gone, the farmers and the field hands, I asked myself this mysterious question.

The gates to the village walls were swaying open. Landseer happened to be right outside. He was fastening the clasp on his horse, tying it down against the strong current in the wind. He had a cart load of paint. I nodded hello and asked what he was doing with all of it. He said he was doing his job of course, under the orders of my father and bringing it to the new castle.

"New castle?" I asked him.

He pointed to the center of town and gruffly said,

"It's right over there. Take a look for yourself. Enstrom and his daughter live there now, as the King's royal bakers."

I looked down the main road in disbelief.
The castle had juristically changed in just a few short
weeks, morphed into a monstrosity of masonry. The
bell tower casted this menacing shadow over the
peoples homes. Looking at it from the right angle
made it appear as if it almost reached the clouds in
the sky. This is what my father was up too, why he
didn't want me around. It was obvious to me then,
he was borrowing the brush without Botticelli's
consent and using it to paint lavish things he didn't
need like he did before.

Landseer told me those showing even the
slightest sign of creativity were immediately
imprisoned without question and all newcomers
were banished until further notice. There was
something off about him, the way he carried himself,
Landseer proclaimed. His mannerisms as if he
wasn't the same man. I knew I had to get inside the
castle and take back control of the brush. I couldn't
allow my father to continue misusing it. Landseer
gladly offered to hide me in his cart and sneak me
inside. I climbed aboard and off we went to the new
castle.

My father waved Landseer in and told him to
unload the paint in the doorway. I began searching
for Botticelli's portrait. The castle had changed so
much since the last time I was there. The ceilings
were higher and bowed, with contouring edges

leading into the empty spaces. At least one of my paintings hung on every wall, next to one of Botticelli's.

In the main hall I found a lavish feast laid out. It had been awhile since I'd eaten a good meal, so I thought I'd grab something to eat. I heard my father waking up from a nap. I almost didn't recognize him. He was sitting at the head of the table in the dark. The shadows in the room consumed his face with the features of an aging old man, mournful of the day's long agenda. I wondered if his illness had returned.

He leaned forward, barely wiping the crumbs off his lips as he spoke with a mouthful of bread,

"My son, I'm surprised to see you so soon. I've had such a hard and tiring week. Come in and sit down, let's regale on your time spent under the stars."

I spouted back, "I've just returned from Grant Wood's. I'd like to talk about that with you if you don't mind."

"And how is my old friend doing?"

"Is it true, did you really give his land to Botticelli?"

My father glared at me in suspicion, "It's the least I could do to show my gratitude toward the man who saved my life, but if you must know. Grant Wood, that ornery old goose, he was happy to give up his farm. Why, what exactly did he tell you?"

"He told me you took it out from under him and he seemed pretty sincere about it. I also ran into Landseer. He said you've requested all the paint in the kingdom."

"Why yes, of course I have. What's there to explain? Botticelli has made a few requests, all I can do is humbly reply. We owe him that much, don't we?"

"I'll agree with you. We do owe him a debt of gratitude, but what does outlawing creativity and banishing newcomers have anything to do with it?"

"Botticelli needs you to be at your best. I can't have your creativity stifled by others, not when the man who saved my life is depending on it."

My father then stuck his thumb in a cherry pie and wiped it on his lips, "Now please, sit down and enjoy this meal with me. Enstrom baked you a pie."

"I won't sit down and stuff my face, not while the people must live under your tyrannical rule."

"Quit being so difficult about things. Your friend Botticelli has given me an extension to my life and I shan't not waste it, neither should you."

My father then stood up and said if I continued undermining his authority he would not have me rule by his side. So I asked who would rule by his side, if not his only son.

He curled his lips together and let out a strong grumble, "You may sit wherever you like, so long as it is not on my throne."

My father stuck his hand in the pie and scarfed down the rest. He then told me to go to my room and he would deal with me later. I left, but where was my room? The only thing I could think of was finding Botticelli and his magic brush. Then maybe I could talk some sense into him.

When I turned the corner I discovered an explosion of artistic dreams, magical murals painted onto the walls of a curved hallway snaking deep into the castle. The fields were beautifully captured in the oils. You could see from one season to the next at a glance. I could feel the warm summer breeze blowing over my face on one side of the wall and the icy winter chill on the other. The impasto moved with the wind, cascading over the landscape. The clouds parasailed into the distant blue voids.

I heard a loud thunderous roar, followed by violent flashes of light. The hallway grew dark for a moment. Then a strong gust of wind blew in a pile of leaves that scattered further into this labyrinth of surreal imagery. There was a storm brewing down the way, I was certain of it.

At the end of the hall was a painting of a room. Though not particularly interesting, I noticed something visually suspicious. There was a doorway left open, peering into a room within a room within a room. Only a master craftsmen could think of something like this, though I couldn't believe it, in my heart I knew all along.

When I opened the last door in the painting, I discovered to my astonishment it was not Botticelli's portrait hanging on the wall, but my father's and he remain quite ill. He told me about Botticelli's lies. How he had imprisoned him in the portrait and spent a whole week painting himself in his image. He planned on taking over and ruling our kingdom, with me by his side as apprentice to his magic. I found the box containing the paintbrush and vowed to my father I would make him pay for what he had done.

Botticelli, the painter entered the room with a crooked smile wiped across my father's face. I picked up the brush and threatened to paint him out of existence if he did not release my father from the canvas. He stood there laughing loudly and arrogantly at my words. So I dipped the brush in paint and made good on my threat, but nothing happened. He took it right out of my grasp, then wiped my father's face from his own, whiskers and all, and ordered that I do as he wishes or suffer from the wrath of his artistic thoughts.

I ran out of the castle and down the main road of town, headed straight for the gates to our once glorious fields. By the time I reached his two fabled hills the sun had nearly vanished. I climbed my way to the top and nestled in with my back propped up against the tree.

Hours later I woke. The stars were all out and yet not one could be seen twinkling in an unnatural way. I wondered if he even cared to bother with me, for it appeared he had what he wanted all along, our once hardworking kingdom under his majestic painter's thumb.

I sat there for the longest time, toiling over how easily I'd been deceived. He took everything from me, the moment he laid that first stroke on the canvas, condemning my father to such a horrible fate. I was naive to think all my problems could be solved so easily. Then I saw a pitchfork and a shovel lying there down below in the fields. I must have forgotten it there last fall, after Botticelli painted all the hard work away. It wasn't much to help, but it was something, no matter how small it was.

I walked down to retrieve them when I noticed the moon, it was acting peculiar, pulsating, forming purple rings around the edges. I picked up the shovel and pulled the pitchfork out of the ground, then I walked back over to the first hill. By then the entire landscape was covered in this mystical fog. I could barley see more than a few yards. So I climbed my way to the top to get a better view of what was going on.

There was a cyclone swirling in the fields, picking up everything it could along the way. It was what I'd worked so hard for over the years, Turnips, carrots, green and red onions, squashes of all shapes and sizes and potatoes with a thousand dead eyes. Oh my! I picked up the shovel and swatted a turnip. I diced a carrot in two with the edge of my shovel. No matter how many came at me, I made sure to eat all of my vegetables.

Now that my foes from the fields had been diced, sliced and planted firmly in the dirt from whence they grew, I picked up an onion and took a hearty bite without so much as shedding a tear.

The hill in front of me then began sinking. I looked down below, the fields were saturated in a black oily mess, devouring the two hills. It was a matter of time before I sank along with it. So I hopped aboard the tree stump and cast off.

Botticelli appeared out of the fog. He was riding atop a horse with the belly of a fish, directing an army of these fire breathing beasts with brush in hand. He was humming off key, a trumpeting score to a march of victory. I scowled at such a tune, but he'd bested me and there was nothing I could do but watch as he made his dreadful approach.

What was left of the two hills, he soaked up into his brush. The horses vanished, as if they were nothing more than a dream. The land returned back to normal and became a field once again for him to choose how he played. The only thing left was the vegetables I ate scattered across the open landscape and his horse which promptly sprouted legs.

The walk home was humiliating for a Prince who once worked hard for his efforts. I was brought to the dungeon and chained to a wall with just a sliver of light to see. There in the opposite corner of my cell was a man sitting humbly in defeat. When he turned his head toward the light I was in shock by what I saw. His face, it lacked distinguishing features, as if they'd been completely wiped clean. Botticelli must have painted them away, erasing any remanence of this man's existence. It left me horrified to think, I wondered if this is what he had in store for me.

The next night Botticelli returned to my cell to ask that I indulge in his dreams.

"Young Ayden, Prince and heir to a pile of dirt. I was growing rather tired of wearing your father's wrinkled face, earned from precious years he so foolishly wasted in the fields. Now that you know the truth, I'll give you a choice. This could all be ours one day, a dream to manipulate together, me as the master and you as my apprentice. Well, what do you say?"

"It would be just that Botticelli, a dream I care not to indulge in."

"Your time in the fields, daydreaming night after night, don't tell me you didn't want more?"

"I only wanted one thing and you've taken that from me."

"Humph! Very well, then live in the squalor and rot in this cell with your new friend. Maybe, after the leaves have fallen and the sight of this man has haunted you long enough, you will change your answer."

Botticelli was just about to leave when I stuck a toting blow to his ego, "Is this how you pay back my father's generosity?"

He smirked discourteously at my words, "To show I am generous, here is the last loaf of bread Enstrom baked, before I ordered his imprisonment for plotting against me, Jared Botticelli, the new king of this castle."

I spent the next month and a half chained to that wall with the words he left me with to ponder on, the last loaf of bread Enstrom baked and my new friend who couldn't hear me sob nightly nor udder a single word to help console me through the darkest time in my life.

Then one night as I was sobbing on as usual, the wall next to me started to crumble. When it gave way, a man wearing a cloak stepped out and stood over me. He removed his hood to reveal a badly scarred and mangled face. Though his eyes were out of proportion and his lips were bent, he looked directly at me when he spoke.

"I am Ethan Bordone of Italy and I carry with a second brush in hopes that you, Prince Ayden of the Kingdom of Fragonard possess the skills necessary to defeat Botticelli and become my father's victor."

I couldn't believe what I was hearing, nor that there would ever be hope I would get a chance to duel with Botticelli. But it was true and this time I might stand a chance in defeating him with a brush of my own. I thought to myself, I would not let him mock me or make a fool of my skill so easily, but alas, it was all a dream. Bordone only carried a little paint with him. Not enough to defeat his magic, but perhaps enough to escape my cell and find where he had hidden the kingdom's paint. Then I could make a painter's palette of my own.

I asked Bordone how he knew where to find me. He said he'd just arrived from a long voyage at sea in search of Botticelli and had heard of my story from a passing villager. I asked he use the last of his paint to remove my chains, so that I may get that chance to avenge our fathers. He said first I had to listen to his tale, for he knew much about the brush and Botticelli's deceitful ways that would help me better understand what I must now face.

...And this young Stefan is the story that he told me.

XI

DANCERS IN BLUE

Fragonard pulled a hanky out of his pocket and shed a few tears inside the canvas.

"Ah – chew! I'm sorry. I'm going to be an oily mess. You will have to excuse me for a moment before I continue. This part of the story always brings me to tears."

"It's alright. I'm sure the story gets better."

"Oh, I'll be fine. My place is here, inside this canvas. Besides, I've had centuries to deal with my fate. The people you meet and the ones who walk by gawking at you make for much laughter later on in the evening."

"I'll bet you gave up all hope when you were locked away."

"No, not all hope. Though I will admit I was feeling quite down on myself. So tell me, do you still feel your dreams are impossible?"

"Well, not impossible I guess."

141

"You guess? Well, what's standing in your way?"

"How do I overcome my father not allowing me to paint? No matter what I do, he won't let me pursue what I love."

"There's a painting that should be hanging up right around the corner in that other room. I often hear people oohing and aweing when they discover such a masterpiece. Why don't you fetch it for me?"

"Okay. What does it look like?"

"It's called, *Peace bringing back abundance.* I would describe it to you, but it should be fairly easy to spot with its vibrant color scheme."

"Alright, hold on and I'll go get it."

Stefan walked around the corner and saw the painting glowing under the museum lights. He pulled it off the hook and then brought it back to the pile.

"Do you want me to lean it against the wall with the others?"

"Yes, please do. Put it in-between Millet and Seurat if you will."

Stefan leaned the painting back and said, "There Fragonard, can you see it?"

"Ah, just fine. What a breathtaking work of art. I haven't seen this painting in almost two-hundred years and yet it hasn't aged a day or lost one ounce of its ambiance."

"So what's so special about this painting?"

"It's not what's special about this piece in particular, though it is quite lovely, but who painted it. Her name was Elisabeth Lebrun. I once hung on a wall in a room full of her portraits. That's how I learned so much about her."

"What's her story anyways?"

"She was ousted during the French Revolution for speaking her mind. Spent nearly twelve years in exile because of it. She continued to paint, despite living life on the lamb. I recall one evening a cannonball went flying through the wall. Almost took out the portrait of one Claude Joseph Vernet, the poor soul."

"She kept painting, even though she had to leave her home."

"Well of course she did. What else would an artist do? If the magic is within you, it isn't something that can be easily shooed away like that fly you bravely hunted down earlier."

"Yeah, but if I go down the path of my father then he'll be happy with me."

"If you follow in his footsteps and do as he says you will succeed just like him and true, he will be happy with you. I don't doubt it. But if you want to pursue your dreams, then you must create your own footprints in the sand. It's as simple as that."

"Yeah, but I don't even know if I'll succeed. I could fail and never become a painter."

"Absurd. If you get knocked down you get back up on that horse and ride again. Just think of the life of Winslow Homer. He was forty-eight when he realized what his true passion was."

"What was his passion?"

"Take a look for yourself. One of his paintings should be hanging up in that other room. Why I would never believe it myself with the descriptions people give. Come to think of it, you'll have to find it on your own."

"How will I know what I'm looking for?"

"I've never heard anyone describe such a painting the way they do this one. It's full of chaos and turmoil. Just follow the raunchy smell of fish-heads and you'll find it."

"I don't think I can smell... uh okay, I'll go look for it."

Stefan wandered into the other room. In the corner there were greyish blue colors swaying at a tilt. It almost spoke to him, the dramatic enchantment of the waves breaking against a boat caught in the crosswinds of a mighty storm. He lifted the painting off the wall and brought it back to Fragonard.

"*The Gulf Stream.* Truly a gift to behold. I can almost taste the salt in the air and feel the warm ocean breeze blowing over my face."

"What about those sharks beneath his feet?"

"Yes, but there is a calm about him, this man struggling to keep for his own. Tally ho! It's as if he's been through this before. It takes time and patience to handle seas as rough as this."

"I don't have the experience he does and I don't want to get eaten by sharks."

"Poor Homer worked twice as hard at something he had no passion for to feed himself throughout his life, but when he finally pursued what he loved, the sea, it didn't seem like work at all."

"I think I understand now."

"So, is there anything else on your mind?"

"Say, while I was over there I saw a painting I really liked."

"Well go and fetch it then. There's no one here to nod their head in objection and tell you otherwise."

"Okay, I'll be right back with it. This one is really cool."

Stefan ran off to go get the painting. He brought it back to Fragonard and leaned it against the wall with the others.

"What a rare find you have there young Stefan. It's an Edgar Degas I believe, *Dancers In Blue.*"

"You've heard of him?"

"Oh why yes. They had an exhibit of his work here back in 1917."

"Do you know anything about him?"

"Degas was a loner. His father pushed him down the path of a lawyer. Try as he may, he just wasn't cut out for that type of work. You can follow in your father's footsteps, but the real you will never get a chance to blossom."

"I don't think I'd be good at anything else. What I mean is I don't think I'd have the same passion as I do when I paint."

"No, you wouldn't. I suppose I should finish with my story now. I seem to have forgotten exactly where I left off, do you happen to recall?"

"I remember you telling me about how your father was really ill and had to be painted onto a canvas. All the kingdoms paint was then placed in a mystical closet and then a magic lock was painted over it. You were locked away, but than you met this mysterious man who said he could help."

"Ah yes, now I remember where I left off..."

148

XII

THE DESPERATE MAN

Listen to my story young Ayden, Prince and heir to the throne of the kingdom of Fragonard, for it is a cautionary tale and one that may help aid you in your battle to defeat Botticelli.

I was a painter once, apprentice to my father who was the King's Royal Painter, a man by the name of Mabuse. My father painted all portraits for our King and his family and he proclaimed he would have no other. Though I was heir to this position of royal importance, I was never quite as good as I claimed to be. I knew if the day so shall arrive he could paint no more, I very well may have been replaced with another. This didn't bother me though, for I was quite happy with the things I painted and the meager living I made at my trade.

Then one day Botticelli arrived in our kingdom. He started spreading a rumor that he was the greatest painter in all the land and that no one rivaled his talents or could compare, including the King's royal painter.

Once word reached my father he became quite enraged to hear of these boastful claims against him. No matter, he knew his royal position was secure, so he blew this off as nothing more than the rhetoric of a desperate man seeking attention and a name for himself.

I didn't think much about this over the course of the next few weeks, but then late one night, just as I was closing up I heard a knock at the backdoor. I peeked through the window to see who it could be. There was an old man with a sunken demeanor standing there. His clothes were full of patches and holes, and his face was badly scarred, as if a mist of scolding hot vapor had sprayed over him. I thought perhaps he was a vagrant who had wandered off from the main part of town. I peered through the glass like a shadow and told him he would find no free meal here at the end of his day.

He was quite persistent to speak with me. He kept banging on the door like a common peddler. So I cracked it open and threw him some day old bread, hoping to persuade him to go elsewhere. He shoved his foot inside and said he wasn't hungry. He was searching for a place that would sell a few of his works of art.

After he told me who he was, I laughed him off with a scoff and told him to go away at once with his claims of surpassing my father as the true master of the brush. He was quick to apologize and explained he was just trying to establish himself as an up and coming artist.

I don't know why I felt pity for this tired old buffoon, despite his pompous arrogance. I said he could come inside and join me for a cup of warm tea. He showed me his paintings, which were beyond compare to anything I'd seen in awhile. The Chardin's and the Murillo's weren't selling as well as they could've been. Frans Hals, one of our more exquisite painters hadn't produced anything sellable in months. In fact, he hadn't painted anything of high quality since *The Laughing Cavalier.* No joking matter about it.

I understood he clearly was a man of rags in need of something in his pockets. I offered to sell a few pieces in an act of charitable kindness. I suppose the rumor he started was the only way he figured he could get his foot in the door to an art gallery. I just asked that he keep the deal between us. I didn't want to upset my father. I was only helping out a fellow artist. I led him out back and said he could sleep wherever he like, so long as he left by morning and didn't return until the moon rose to its highest peak.

The next morning however, I discovered to my dismay he was still asleep in our backyard. I thought I'd made myself perfectly clear. We had neighbors to think about who weren't going to put up with this sort of nonsense. He rolled over and hid his eyes from my discerning view. I poked him in the back a few times and told him I wasn't running a brothel. He slowly got on his feet and demanded that I feed him something. I gave him an apple out of the basket and said he could eat it at the park.

Before he left he told me of some fine bristles that he carried with and asked if I'd turn them into a paintbrush. I didn't make my own, but there was a painter down the street by the name of Raeburn, an old friend of my father's. He was perhaps the finest brush-maker in town. I said if he were to visit there to mention my name and for a small fee he would make him a more than adequate brush.

After he left I decided to myself this would be the last dealings I would have with this ragged beggar man, once he picked his things up at the end of the night.

My father showed up at the galleria later on. He looked over the new paintings and asked where I discovered such marvelous work. I told him about a man visiting from another kingdom that asked if I could sell his paintings to pay for his travels. My father insisted on meeting with this mysterious artist.

He was curious to learn more about him and his unusual yet immaculate technique for displaying such bright, vivid colors on the canvas. I explained how unfortunately he had to leave on some urgent matters, but I would talk with this stranger whom we did not know.

When night fell Botticelli returned with a smile on his face, for he carried with a box that contained his new paintbrush and the fate of our two kingdoms. He asked for his pay, another cup of tea and that he might be able to spend one more night amongst the flowers in our backyard. With the money I'd just given him, I assured him he'd be able to find an inn with a vacant room. Thankfully, he left without any more qualms.

The next day he returned a filthy mess, as if he'd been sleeping in the woods. Because of his consistent odor problems and ragged attire, I told him I could no longer sell his work. He didn't bother arguing the point, as I assume most of his life he had to deal with the consequences of his subservient way of living. Though looking back on it now, my words with him may have been a little harsh.

Just as he was on his way out my father met him at the door. Botticelli introduced himself and apologized for mocking his skill. My father admitted after viewing his work, there was much to be envious of, though I think he was just trying to be polite. He sat Botticelli down and asked if he was interested in becoming a regular painter at our galleria. I should have contested right then and there. My father was so infatuated by the man I decided to let him see for himself what a crude unkempt person he truly was.

Botticelli accepted his offer and for the next few months I had to put up with him sleeping on the flowers in our backyard. The rhododendron had the hardest time in dealing with him. Why I don't believe they ever recovered. He mostly kept to himself and generally worked at night. Though I rarely saw him, I was displeased with his laziness. My father never complained, for his paintings, when he produced them always fetched a fair sum of money.

Then one day the King announced he was throwing a ball for my father's birthday. I wore this fine feathered cap and buckled shoes with these beautiful gaping bows on them. Oh and a dashing blue cape to go with my ensemble.

I applied a few droplets of perfume and adjusted my hat. All I had to do now was stop by the galleria to pick up a painting called *The Lovers.* It was a gift for the King's daughter, Eleanor Siddal. Sometime during the party, after adorning her with gift upon gift professing my love, my true intentions, I was going to ask for that dance I so longed to have with her over the years. Oh well, nonetheless I am here now telling you this story wearing the rags of my impairment.

When I entered the back room Botticelli asked why I was dressed so finely. I told him the King was throwing a party of course. I thought every one knew. Upon hearing this news, he pleaded to go with. He even asked if I would introduce him to the king. I couldn't believe he would ask such an absurd question. Why the king only met with those who had worked hard to earn and secure their stature, certainly not someone of his means.

I let out a chortling snort and said, "With the way you often dress, I doubt the king would even allow you to pick through the garbage for scraps at such a grand event."

He was rather upset by my reply, but he needed to understand something. I had a girl to impress with my charm and wit. It was proper protocol and I couldn't be bothered by his inability to comprehend the obvious. So I ignored his foolish hopes in life and went to the party without giving it a second thought.

Someone once asked me if it is better to be callous in the mind or careless with the heart. In this case, I chose to be mindful of the whole situation.

XIII

THE BOY BLUE

On my way into the party I ran into my old friend Maes whom I hadn't seen in years. He told me every royal painter from across the land was invited. They would be presenting their grandest works of art as a surprise to pay tribute to my father's talents, a skill envied by all artists of the day. I was somewhat relieved Botticelli would not be attending. His presence would've brought on much embarrassment for my father and me.

Sure enough, when I entered the ballroom some of the most exquisite painters had already arrived. Greuze, Lawrence, Boucher, Perroneau and Watteau to name a few. Oh and Reynolds was there as well. I was a bit surprised to see him, what with Gainsborough's presence across the hall. The two had a long standing rivalry, but over matters that are none of my concern or yours.

What a wondrous event and even more wondrous still, I heard the most delightful little melody playing in the backdrop. The King hired Metsu, truly the finest musician ever heard by someone with two ears and a desire to listen. The King's daughter, Eleanor Siddal, she was swaying to this waltzing anthem of wealth and taste by her lonesome self. I'll never forget what she wore, though it was tailored in the wrong size. It was the most ravenous yellow buttercup evening gown, with all the frills and frollies you could think of.

She made a turn, we locked eyes and then she went the other way. That's when I knew this was my chance to see if she cared to dance. I made my way toward her, navigating through a sea of lace and ribbon. Ah, but before I even had my chance, she vanished into a cloud of satin and silk embroidery. The momentum of the music picked up and so this innocent little game of cat and mouse was on.

After the music died down I found her out on the balcony. She was with her two best friends Kiki and Dora Maar. I asked if she had a moment to spare. I promised I wouldn't bother her the rest of the evening. Her two friends quickly walked off, laughing at who knows what, perhaps the gossip of the day.

Now that the two of us were alone I got down on one knee and removed a letter from within my inside pocket, speaking words of love flowing from the heart that I'd never dared to utter to her before.

"When I'm with you I feel like we're climbing a mountain and when we reach the top, day turns into night and the stars and moon come out only to reveal your beautiful, radiant soul. When the sun rises and dawn breaks, the day becomes brighter with each smile, each look that you give me. You are my young love, my new love, my old love, my soulmate."

Etcetera, etcetera, etcetera. In reality I was never that good at expressing how I truly felt with a pen. I bought the poem from a man by the name of Rossetti. He was well known as a brazen man of song and lyric who knew how to speak directly from the heart. I was sure his words would surrender her to my arms without hesitation.

To my surprise, after professing my true intentions she ran back into the party without saying a single word in response to my linguistic bravado. Any man would have given up hope, but I kept hope alive just in case there was that chance.

I followed after in this amorous pursuit of love, but she was nowhere in sight, not even from a sparrows hidden view. I checked by Metsu's orchestra, hoping she was waiting to take my hand in a waltz around the room, but she wasn't there either. I wondered if this wasn't all but a mere requiem of my lustful desires, until I heard a voice trying to sequester silence over the crowd.

The music stopped abruptly. Everyone turned their heads and looked down the center aisle, as the King was about to speak. I was concerned that I may have come on a bit strong with his daughter, but to my unexpected joy he announced our marriage. I guess our little talk on the balcony was misunderstood as a proposal of love ever after. Eleanor was blushing red with excitement. The way her eyes marveled brightly under the lights as if she was about to faint, let me know I'd found true love.

This was turning out to be a grand event for the Bordone's. Love was in the air. The music, the mood, the people. I couldn't have been happier and neither could my father. I was not only heir to the position of Royal Painter, but now I was heir to the throne as well or so one would assume I think.

The King then made another surprise announcement. He left the task of judging the works of art on display to my father and me. The winner receiving the position of heir to my father's seat at the King's table and as an added bonus a dance with Eleanor as the last dance she would ever have with another man before taking my hand.

Now I really had to pick wisely, for whomever won this prize would get a chance to dance with the love of my life.

My father started the competition off by weeding out the weak, separating the fine art from the rubbish. After inspecting their work, discussing the composition, palette and overall subject matter, he left me with a ménage `a trois between only the finest standing in the room. Lawrence, Gainsborough and Maes were all that was left. What a worthy group of masters to choose from. You could hear a pin drop in the crowd, as I carefully passed judgement on their work.

The first piece I reviewed was by Gainsborough. He already had a standing with the Royal line. His painting of *The Boy Blue* however displayed far too much wealth and old money. One should be mindful when choosing symbols of their stature or it could come back to haunt you. So I moved onto the next painting to see what sort of character it reflected in my own.

Maes brought with a humbling piece called, *The Idle Servant.* It was a depiction of two woman cleaning up in the kitchen after a dinner party. One of them had fallen asleep, the other, an older woman was standing over her, glaring in disapproval. It was a wonderful gesture towards a King seeking the approval of those less-fortunate in our kingdom. I carefully considered announcing him as the winner, but I still had one more piece to review.

161

The last painting, *Pinkie Girl* by Lawrence garnered some favorable attention from the crowd. It was an affectionate piece that truly celebrated the mood of the evening. The innocence of this beautiful young girl depicted on the canvas, holding her hand near her heart submissively to the will of the taker. She had an unbreaking gaze peering into the eyes of her future lover, whomever that may be.

Ah, but before I could begin toiling over these masterpieces, Eleanor said she'd already made up her mind. She fancied Lawrence's work over the other two. So I announced him as the winner. The crowd applauded pleasingly with my decision. The King then gave the dance with his daughter to Lawrence, for appeasing her tastes and my eye. He was the last one I wanted to dance with her, but of course. If only you knew the King like I did. Well, I couldn't begin to question his word, once it had been spoken. That would just be silly.

Finally, it was my turn to unveil the gift I brought for Eleanor. My father proclaimed it really wasn't necessary. I insisted he allow me to display my love for Eleanor before the world. I removed the drape disguising this masterpiece in the making and revealed a work of art simply titled, *The Lover's.* Everyone burst out in barbaric laughter. My father hid his eyes in shame. They said it was just a bunch of flat, tonal shapes and that it wasn't actually art.

What do they know? I could tell Eleanor was rather upset with the crowd. She quickly covered the painting and demanded we carry on with the festivities.

The King ordered the crowd silenced so Metsu could begin a performance of his called, *The Music Lesson*. While Eleanor and Lawrence were waltzing playfully to a lover's serenade I drew dreadfully tired of the party. There's only so much pomp and circumstance one can put up with in an evening. So I decided to go to the galleria and see what Botticelli was up too.

To be honest, after spending all that time with him, I suppose he was finally starting to grow on me, the way unwanted flies grow on a green apple.

I found him in the backroom blending a hue together. He was finishing up the final touches on another portrait, one of many he'd been painting lately. It had been an obsession with him. I don't know why he even bothered. It was a waste of time and talent if you ask me. Most artists usually only painted a portrait when someone had commissioned them to do so.

After he applied the veneer over the lips of some poor unlucky fellow who had his brow ridge painted a little too high, he put his brush down and asked why I wasn't still at the party. Oh, I don't remember exactly what it was I said to him. I gave him some excuse.

He asked if I cared to go for a walk. I thought it was a splendid idea and suggested we go for a stroll through Ruben's Garden or perhaps sit on a bench in Hobbema Park for awhile and feed the ducks. They'd just put in a new pond, larger than the last one, though I suppose not as eloquent. He didn't seem all that enthusiastic about my ideas.

There was a place on the other side of town where many of his artistic friends frequented. He said he had some business affairs to take care of there. After that, we could go where ever I pleased. I assumed all the artists in the kingdom were at the ball celebrating my father's birthday. I guess not everyone could attend. Against my better judgement I took him up on his offer and so we went on a walk there instead.

I met quite a few interesting, yet awkwardly displaced people on this walk. Many of them impoverished, with a tale of woe to tell. It was sad really. They never found a way to pull themselves up from the situation they put themselves in.

We met this one fellow, Paul Cézanne was his name. I stopped and talked to him for awhile. He was a quarry worker, I could tell. His hands truly showed their age. He didn't seem like the type who cared much for what stature one held or how one presented themselves.

I remember meeting another man by the name of Marcel Duchamp. He was playing a game of chess.

"To serve the mind, rather than the eye," is what he said to himself over and over again.

The poor soul seemed so disheveled and beaten down by his personal atrocities. I had to turn the cheek and look on.

This one man was sitting alone in an alleyway, plucking the strings of a violin under the light of his candle. He played the saddest tune I ever heard. Botticelli said his name was Georges Braque, an unappreciated musician who lost his job a few months back due to a decree signed by the king. I didn't want to get political, I told him and so we counited to roam the streets.

We turned down the next corner and there were people dancing and laughing, having a good time. The music was delightfully charming, more so than a boring old waltz. It had an upbeat tempo, savage and primal, echoing the rhythm of eternity. The bass sounded like a bottled up baboon beating its chest in aggression. The trombone wailed like an elephants trunk and the guitar fought with the tenacity of a raging bull.

In the center of this cabaret was a daring woman in a lovely tattered blue dress. She wasn't wearing any shoes, but that didn't seem to stop her from hopping around the crowd, pulling a suitor out she fancied with a glint of her eyes. Oh they were majestic. Beautifully lined in dark blue and satin. I so wanted to join in on the fun, but I didn't think a girl like her would be interested in someone like me. Then, as she made her next turn, she grabbed onto my hand and yanked me out in the middle. I didn't have a clue as to what I was doing. I just followed her step and she did the rest.

When the music changed tempo we took a rest on a bench away from the crowd. She introduced herself as Tintoretta, the little dyer girl, as she rested her hand on my shoulder. I have to say I was quite smitten, but unfortunately I'd just been engaged to the king's daughter. I didn't think Eleanor would approve of such scandalous behavior of me. She said not to worry, for she'd met men like me before, though I don't believe I'd ever met a woman like her.

The music picked up again and so she continued to frolic for their amusement, while I wandered down the street to go and find Botticelli at that pub.

There wasn't a sign above the door, but I could hear people on the inside hollering like feral, bovine creatures. I pinched my nose and stepped into to a wild party of drunken ne'er-do-wells. Ugh. It stank of a roosters den.

Botticelli was at a table playing a gambling game with cups. I think that was the business affairs he claimed he had to attend to so urgently. It seemed he had a knack for this game or rather a trick up his sleeve that allowed to do so well. I sat down at the bar. I didn't want to lose all my money in such a frivolous way.

These two gentleman sat down on either side of me and proposed quite an interesting question with a hiccup and a burb.

"Excuse me young lad. You seem like an intellectual type, with your feathery blue ensemble. My friend Chagall and I were discussing something. Perhaps you could enlighten us."

"I don't know if I can, but I'll certainly try my best." I replied.

The man stuck his finger in the air and said, "Tell me, is art a dream shared by all or is it only something for those who wish to see it?"

His friend interrupted before I even had a chance to reply, "No, no. You misunderstood me to begin with Matisse. I believe what my friend is trying to say, there is always art present, but not all can admire nor appreciate the beauty in a flower. Wouldn't you agree to this quandary?"

"What is there to agree on Chagall? It is a question, not a statement. Let the man answer."

I didn't think the two of them would stop arguing. So I decided to propose a thought provoking statement of my own to add to the conversation.

"Should art only be confined to the canvas or can it be defined by shapes rather than the absolute boundaries we conceive."

"Why not? Good answer, Sir. Let's toast to it. So you propose that the dream is shared by all, but rather not defined by one's definition."

"No, wrong again. What the lad was trying to say is, defined by ones question. Isn't that so?"

I'd never had such an enlightening conversation with a fellow artist before. All the artists at the party wanted to talk about were who commissioned their last work and the dowry they received. There was little talk of pushing the boundaries of what art really is or could be. I found myself immersed in their world, though I'd never been to this side of town.

I was about to propose another thought provoking question, when Botticelli was thrown right into the middle of our conversation. The bartender said to take it out back, he wasn't going to put up with anymore ruff housing in his establishment. They picked Botticelli up and threw him out the backdoor into the alleyway. My new friends told me not to bother. He'd been thrown out that door plenty and always managed to come out ahead. I just couldn't sit there while he was being accosted, so I went to see what all the fuss was about.

When I opened the back door one of the men rolled up his sleeve, revealing a tattoo of a dragon. It had a tail that spiraled around his arm almost endlessly in a hypnotic whorl. Botticelli didn't hesitate. He pulled out his brush and palette and painted the dragon off his forearm. He then sent it chasing after him for what was once a mere thoughtless doodle.

I was in complete awe by this unbelievable feat. After those ruffians were out of sight, he withdrew the dragon and wrapped it on his own arm to use it upon our kingdom at a later time. Who knew this dragon was a mystery written on the wall foretelling the future of what was to become of me?

We left the alleyway and continued wandering the streets like a couple of jesters at the king's ball. I remember we walked by Moroni's tailor shop, a place that sold higher end fabrics. I suggested with his winnings he visit there in the morning and turn his rags in for something more suited to the likings of a King and his Royal Court. He looked at me with an uneasiness of disapproval. I told him to cheer up and that tomorrow, once he acquired his new attire, he just might feel better about himself. He thought perhaps I was right and then he threw a rock in the window and started doing some late night shopping.

I waited for him outside and when he returned, he was wearing some fine black attire and a long and billowy hat that matched that crooked smile of his.

Botticelli and I then walked back to the galleria. I helped him lay down on the flowers in our backyard. He asked that I sit with him for awhile and gaze upon the stars. I thought that was a rather silly idea, lying about in the dirt while we waste our time staring up at the sky. I decided to go inside and take a nap in the galleria like a civilized human being. He kept rambling on. He even asked about my dreams in life. What an absurd question and he had many of them. I'm an artist, not one of those idealists types who lives their life idly from one moment to the next.

One can't hope all their problems will be solved simply by wishing for them in their dreams. He then offered to paint my portrait, as a token of our friendship. I explained I already had enough painted by my father hanging on the walls of the King's castle and I didn't need anymore.

It's a good thing I declined his offer or I might be telling you this story from within the confines of a canvas. In life sometimes you must ignore the persistence of the lonely. So that's what I did about it. By the time I had my hand on the handle I think he got the picture.

XIV

PORTRAIT OF AN ARTISAN

The next day my head was throbbing like an orangutang. I thought the night before was a delusional dream brought on by too much gale laughter and red punch had at the party, then I noticed some new attire hanging on Botticelli's desk chair. The events from there slowly began to unravel, the encounter with that daring woman, those ruffians Botticelli got into a scuffle with at the bar. I specifically recalled him throwing a rock into a shop window. I couldn't remember the name of the place, but I was sure he threw that rock.

When I confronted him about it, he said a tailor by the name of Moroni fell in love with a painting of his, *Portrait of the Artists Son*. He just had to have it, but he fell short on the price tag. So he traded him for the clothes. He hoped his new attire would garner the favor he sought with our higher end cliental.

Of course that was a lie and he often gave that up with a crude breath of air, followed by a whining snivel.

While I was trying to piece things together my father showed up. To my surprise, he presented Botticelli with a painting entitled, *La Primavera*. It was well done, not one of his typical motifs of royalty standing in a noble pose or the barbarism of gladiators caught in the heat of the moment. I remember these surreal like creatures depicted on it. They were gathered in some sort of enchanted forest scene, performing a ritual by the looks of it.

My father said it was his way of thanking him for producing such fine work over the past few months. He said everything about the piece reminded him of how he only painted at night and daydreamed of his fairytale inspired masterpieces during the day. Botticelli thanked him and said he had a gift for him in mind as well, a late birthday present. He offered to paint his portrait. My father thought it was a splendid idea, to have a likeminded master capture his essence on a canvas and it was settled as easy as that. His fate was sealed forever with a crooked smile and a handshake with the devil himself.

They got started sometime in the late evening. My father was waiting patiently in front of an unusually wide and tall canvas propped up on an easel. He was posed nobly as he would have anyone of his own subjects do. I didn't realize he planned on painting his entire stance, but I suppose that's what they agreed on.

Botticelli laid out his paints, every shade down to the whiskers. He began with a stroke of paint over his garments and then he swiped them onto the face of the canvas, quite literally. I was completely unaware. I guess I just didn't want to believe what I was seeing. No matter. I can't change the events of the past, I can only live with the regret of the future.

I grew tired of the ramblings of these two old men crooning on about the study of cadavers, muscle tendons, hamstrings and arteries and so on. So I went out back and took a nap on Botticelli's bed of flowers. Some time after the stars came out I woke thinking they had left, perhaps gone to that bar Botticelli took me to. Then I heard this muffled sound coming from the corner of the room, behind the canvas.

To my utter horror, when I turned the painting over I found my father bound to it like a strong horse glue. It was an exacting replica of the man, the grey streaks running through his beard, his pronounced brow and cheek bones. It was almost like looking into a mirror, aged fifty years or so or I don't know. Oh. He's old.

My father remained strong. He told me of Botticelli's plot to overthrow his seat next to the King's and how he was planning on overthrowing the King's seat as well. I told him to wait there in the painting and I would go to the King at once and explain everything.

Then I looked around the room at all those portraits Botticelli had been painting lately. Their eyes followed my every move. The situation was earnestly dire, more than I realized. They were alive, yet frozen in time, their lips sealed with a thick coat of veneer. All our best clients, El Greco, the Bellini brothers, Durer and De Hooch. Hobbema as well. Oh, the poor soul. He just had a new pond named in his honor, all of them condemned by the strokes of his brush. The laughing cavalier was hysterical with laughter over the whole inconvenient situation.

Botticelli then burst open through the front door. He said I would not escape the night alive, unless I promised to sit still and share my father's fate inside the canvas. I told him he was a fool and when the King found out about his treachery, he would have him hunted down and hanged for what he had done. Botticelli chased me out the back door and that's when he painted my face into this Picasso of a mess you see before you Fragonard.

I didn't have a mirror, but I could feel what he had done to me by merely placing my hands over this disproportionate mess. I became the *Portrait of an Artisan,* a blank canvas for him to choose how he used the devious strokes of his brush. I ran away from his harrowing laughter, the effulgence of his crooked smile, crimson oily tears washing over the paleness of my blue cheeks in shades of violet and lavender. Botticelli followed after, paintbrush in hand, ready to finish the job.

I made a dash for it down the alleyway and got lost in a jungle of backstreets. The orientation of the foreground and the background melded into one, as I was not yet accustom to my new eyes. The buildings shifted out of alignment, analytically broken down and then re-constructed to produce something hauntingly unreal.

This heinous spell he placed over me did strange things to my other senses as well, altering my perception of not only sight, but even touch, smell, sound and speed were distorted to an exaggeration of the truth. It also gave me multiple viewpoints on every object I came into contact with. My understanding of space, volume and mass was reduced to a symbolic representation in its purist form.

I saw some lights flickering in the windows up ahead. There was a cabaret of gypsies with their tents all set up. They were entertaining the crowd with jugglers and fire breathers and chance games. I thought someone would see I was in danger and offer to lend a helping hand.

I quickly got lost in the crowd. It wasn't difficult to blend in. I looked like a clown to be mocked and heckled.

A one-eyed strong man yelled, "Watch where you're going." as I bumped into him, his voice strident and forceful.

I could feel his aggression flowing through my body as if though I were a translucent being made of light and air.

The harlequins and Pierrot performers acted as mosaics, sculpted motifs of clay, twisted and contorted, the mechanical motion of human beings.

This little boy was wandering aimlessly through the crowd. He was looking for its "Dada" It was irrational nonsense. What did the child mean?

Screaming monsters to my insomnia, indifferent to my problems. Was I so far detached from these people that they could not see the humanity in me?

Botticelli spotted me from across the square. I ran back into the alleyways to try and lose him. He remained right behind me, hot on my tail.

I yelled out, "Why have you done this to me? Hasn't my father and I provided you with an affordable living?" my voice burrowed and rattled against the brick and mortar.

Botticelli scowled back, "Consider your face a fitting pun Bordone, for someone who squandered his life in the shadow of his father." his voice vibrating in disillusionment.

"How dare you mock me. I was only trying to live up to his good name." The sound of my own voice moved throughout the night, breaking in unusual patterns.

The treble in his laughter grew louder, the vibrancy of his tone reverberating into lines, his footsteps collating in washes of muddy puddles. The Stone Beat Jungle. The vibrations led to a wash of yellowish green down a narrow passageway. It was the light from the streetlamps breaking in-between the buildings.

I ended up at a four-way stop on the corner of Theotokópoulos Boulevard and Schiele Street. The glow from the streetlamps fused with the darkness in shards of shattered glass. The road moved in circular waves, arcing in bounding rings, swaying side to side with the movement of his beguiling voice. I realized than I could no longer escape his deceitfully crooked smile. I tried pleading with his compassionate side, but found there was none to be had by this madman haunting my reality.

I fell to my knees, cowering in the middle of the street, my eyes hidden from view. "Please, get it over with. Finish the job you started. I no longer want to have to bear through this curse you have placed inside of me anymore."

His shadow towered over me, as well as his words, "Fair enough Bordone. I will see to it you and your father are mine forever to do with as I please on an easel. The King shall soon follow and his throne, his lavish living and his arrogance shall be mine as well!"

Botticelli raised his brush in the air, the light wallowing in the shallowness of his features, ready to strike me down and forever paint me away. Out of nowhere I heard his name shouted loud in anger. I thought it was another distorted noise, altered by my perception of reality, then I rubbed my eyes to see things more clearly. All I was able to make out was a series of unintelligible shapes. Then I heard his voice again.

There was a mob carrying buckets of paint marching down the street. They doused him with everything they had in an attempt to dispel his evil magic. The poor souls didn't even know how powerful he'd become. Botticelli didn't hesitate. He painted that tattoo right off his arm into a one-hundred, no a two-hundred, no a five-hundred-foot paint breathing nightmare and not a thimble more.

The people scattered throughout the back alleyways as the dragon spewed its fiery temper in a thousand different shades. I ran into the confusion. Though I wasn't sure where I was going with my sight continuing to get worse, out of nowhere a hand of compassion reached out and pulled me to safety. My exhausting night in the streets was finally over. It was Tintoretta, the girl I met outside of the pub. She rushed me upstairs to her loft above Moroni's tailor shop. Thank the stars and moon above I ran into her that night.

We stayed up and talked for hours on end about all kinds of philosophical things. She was quite the conversationalist. I remember this large fresco she had displayed on the ceiling. *The Origin of the Milky Way.* It was a marveling wonder of achievement, the way the colors splashed over the starry scenery of the heavens above. The hours she must have spent dedicated to this single work of art and it was just casually on display in her living room.

She said she painted it late one night when she swore the stars were moving in an unusual manner. I had no idea she was a painter. Oh if I wasn't infatuated with her before, I certainly was now.

I thought the piece would fit in nicely with the ones on display in the King's castle. That is, if I put in a good word on her behalf. She laughed and said the King already asked if she wanted to become a Court Painter. She said she turned down the offer because her father wouldn't allow his daughter to paint strictly for the wealthy.

To hear, the King, he actually thought so fondly of another he would even dare entertain the very idea of having a painting hang on his walls that was not crafted under the Bordone name.

Our conversation made me rethink a few things I thought I once knew about myself. I began to look at life through a new set of eyes, tandem and brown. The one feature on my face Botticelli left untouched. Though they're out of place, you can still see the glimmer in them Tintoretta was so fond of. She was a daring woman to befriend me. I will never forget her or the many others I met on my travels.

In the morning, after she washed out the stains and splatters of paint on my garments, I sought out my old friend Raeburn...

Bordone leaned down and gave Fragonard a nudge on the shoulder, "Fragonard, are you awake?"

"Ugh – umm. Yes Bordone. I'm awake, what is it?"

"It appeared you dozed off for a moment. I'm not boring you, am I? The caliber of my brow hasn't put you to sleep? Oh I hope this isn't so. I've been told I tend to ramble when I get excited."

"No, of course not. I was just resting my eyes. Go on, I've been listening. You were telling me something about how you and Botticelli were up late at night enjoying a cup of warm tea?"

"Yes, yes. Anyways, we talked and talked, about life, music, painting. We even talked about the weather, if you can believe that. Ha!"

"Shush – Bordone, you're rambling. I mean, I think I hear Botticelli coming."

"I wonder what that dastardly snake could possibly want?"

"It doesn't matter. Tuck yourself away behind the wall until he leaves. Then we'll continue talking."

"Alright, I'll just be behind this wall hiding away from the world and all the problems that have forsaken me."

"Bordone."

"Oh, yes. Right."

Botticelli then entered the room just as Bordone tucked himself behind the wall.

"Good evening Fragonard. You still persist in holding a conversation with this forgotten memory of my past. I could remove him entirely, brick by brick to fill in that hole, but let him be a reminder of what happens when you cross paths with a master."

"Did you come down here just to pester me or is there a purpose to your vile visit?"

"I have some unfortunate news. Your friend Logan Landseer was thrown from his horse the other day. He died early this morning from the fall.."

"How could you let him die! Did his kindness mean nothing to you?"

"Landseer was one of the few in your kingdom I did admire for his skills. He certainly was a fine craftsmen, but he refused my help. Said he wouldn't be healed by a charlatan with a deceitfully crooked smile as beautiful as mine."

"Before others circum to your treachery Botticelli, release my father from the canvas and the rest of the people you've imprisoned down here since you started this madness."

"I will release them, if you but make one simple promise to me. Apprentice under my magic and skills as a painter or share in your father's fate inside the canvas. Well, what shall it be?"

"I believe the answer is obvious. If you have any dignity left, you could paint this man a face or at least a brow, so that I may receive a proper response when I speak of your ill will."

"Since you enjoy his companionship, then the least I could do is tell you his name. After all, you wouldn't want to address him improperly when introducing him to others."

"How dare you, of course not. I've always given proper introductions. Now tell me his name and do not mispronounce it! So that I may address him proper when speaking to others."

"Raeburn, the last man to stand in my way. Now, if you will excuse me. It is nearing dark and I have some flowers in the garden that need attending."

After Botticelli left the room, Bordone came out from behind the wall with tears running down his colorful, pale blue cheeks.

"Oh Fragonard. I did not know it was Raeburn. Poor Raeburn. He does not deserve this. His magic knows no bounds. See to it you give him the justice he has not afforded us. He truly is a madman who will do anything within his power to get to the top, so long as he does not have to work hard for his efforts."

"That I can agree on. Now finish telling me your story, so I may begin my final battle with this monster and show him the true skills of a master who knows how to wield the brush properly."

"Just promise me you will let him know I gave you the brush and who it was crafted under."

Bordone then put a hand on his disproportionately blue chin and told Fragonard the rest of his story.

"Now let me see, where did I leave off? Oh yes, I remember now. Poor Raeburn, the last time I saw him..."

XV

OFF VALPARAISO

...The two of us were *Off Valparaiso*. I suppose I should start from the beginning. I had just left Tintoretta's home above Moroni's tailor shop and began on my walk to the Galleria. If I was to have Botticelli arrested, then I needed proof of what he had done to my father so I could present it before the King.

I was constantly heckled, ridiculed by the people I passed on the street. They laughed at me and called me mean names, but I was not a monster. At least not on the inside, anymore. I stopped and fell to my knees in pitiful blue shame. I was feeling profoundly depressed and cheerless.

There in a puddle in the street I caught a glimpse of my face, what he had done with it. I stared in disbelief, as the ripples washed over the reflection of my gruesome looks. The nature of my reality had been forever changed. My emotions off balance, tittering on the edge of reason. It evoked something within, producing something without. I had manifested into a metaphorical figure, replaced with only the defects of my character. However I felt about it, what I saw is what I knew to be there all along. No edge, no transparency, no real tangible truth, just a question I began to ponder on,

"Was life imitating art or was the art imitating me?"

I couldn't help but think of the life I once led and the embellished snobbery of my new nose. One eye rose whereas the other fell under the chalky velvet lining of my brow. My heart morns tearfully a deep enriched shade of cobalt blue. The worst of it is when I blush. The pigments in my cheeks shine in an embarrassing rosy red hue. I wondered if the face I once wore was my disguise and this is what was truly underneath, a narrowminded collage of my tormented soul.

I looked into a window to see what was once layered deep, without the water distorting what had become of me. There was a sign in the windowsill with the King's insignia on it. It was a decree informing the fate of our aristocratic community. It was quite obvious an artist of the eclectic variety was the culprit behind all of this and the King was furious. I don't blame him one bit, yet part of me felt he was overreacting.

On the other hand, Botticelli placed a permanent mark on our kingdom. The uneven streets, the giant dead butterfly, the hazy mist of flowers fluttering freely about. Not to mention the splotches of color splattered everywhere by that paint breathing tattoo on his arm. It was all the people could talk about. They demanded swift justice be dealt.

This is what the decree said as I sobbed on and read.

Since the colorful events of the night before have left my kingdom in such a frantic state of emergency, I, King Mabuse, hereby put into effect the following laws. First and foremost, all painters, daydreamers and aristocratic thinkers of this nature alike are hereby banished. I shall give you until one hour after the sun has risen to leave. Ships shall be waiting down by the docks to take you wherever you wish to go, so long as it is nowhere near my dominion. Second, all paints, shades and hues, if not removed by this time shall be commandeered and put to a flame. So I suggest you take them with you. Thirdly, anyone who shows even the slightest hint of an eccentric nature shall be promptly arrested without question and hanged the following day.

Sincerely, King Mabuse

What a terrible fate to befall upon our aristocratic community. To think, what would become of a society without the freethinkers that make it a tolerable place to live?

This however was my chance to finally catch him. I knew he would be leaving on one of those ships in the morning. That meant I only had a little time left as well to gather some things and leave, if the portrait of my father did not save my neck with the King.

I rushed to the galleria hoping to find my father, only to discover Botticelli had ransacked the place. I thought to myself, I should've never given that man the time of day and I should have never allowed him to sleep so comfortably in our backyard. I suppose now I have to consider it a lesson learned and well learned at that about those seeking a free meal at the end of their day.

I searched everywhere for my father's portrait, but found nothing in return. I assumed Botticelli must have decided to take it with him to hold it against me. The only thing he left behind was his dirty rags. The stench was unbearable!

Most of the paintings were tilted and covered in gobs of paint, much like my face. Then I noticed this work of art still hanging up amidst the chaos. It was a piece called *Hope* done by a fellow named

Watts. The painting was of a somber blind woman strumming the strings of her harp. I never understood what it meant to the artist, but at that moment it meant something to me. I wiped the tears from my pitiful blue shame and decided I would find a way to defeat him.

Though I still had no idea how to combat against his evil magic, with the help of the only real friend I ever had, I was sure I would stand a chance. I just hoped old Raeburn could see that it was me behind the mask I must now wear. I showed up on his doorstep late in the evening. He thought I was a crazed lunatic at first, the way I rambled on. He actually threw me some day old bread, as if I were a common peddler searching for some scraps to gnaw on.

Once he figured out who I was, he quickly rushed me inside. I told him everything that happened. He may not have believed a word of it, but I guess the colorful patchwork that makes up this face said it all. He offered his home for the night and promised he would stay by my side, until we found a way to restore this Picasso of a mess and undo my father's fate.

During our conversation he told me something that gave me a newfound confidence we would bring that no good charlatan to justice.

Apparently, Raeburn had one upped Botticelli without even realizing it. When he brought those magical bristles to him, he rather snidely told him to put it on my father's tab. This didn't sit well with old Raeburn, as you can imagine. So he took it upon himself to make a second brush for full payment of services rendered.

The next morning we rushed off down by the docks to try and stop him. Just as we arrived, Botticelli climbed aboard a ship and cast off. We were told it was already filled to its capacity with great works of art and paint galore. I asked where the ship was headed. I was told somewhere near Valparaiso. I knew, if we were ever going to catch him we needed to secure our own ship with many sails and fast. There was only one left down by the docks.

As we made our way to the last ship, I ran into the King and his daughter Eleanor Siddal, the love of my life. They asked if I'd seen Bordone or his son Ethan. I was told if I knew of their whereabouts, I would be pardoned from the rulings of the decree. They didn't recognize me at all. In fact, Eleanor couldn't bear to look. Her eyes were somewhere else. Lawrence, that Finkelstein rat. He was there consoling her for her grief. I'll admit. I was quite upset, but I really felt it was the right thing to do. To leave the love of my life and the King, waiting down by the docks in search of something they would never find there anyways.

We met a man by the name of Somerscales who introduced himself as the captain. I thought that was rather obvious and unnecessary to mention. He was wearing the right attire after all. He asked where we would like to set sail, since it was being paid for by the King. I pointed out across the long lay of the sea and told him not lose sight of that ship at any cost. He asked if I had a vendetta with their captain, a stout and burly man by the name of Manet. I tried explaining to him how Botticelli had permanently scarred my face, but he didn't seem to care. Said he'd sailed with men far uglier than me and offered up his services without hesitation.

Personally, I think he was looking for an excuse to go on an adventure. That's how all the sailors of our kingdom acted, with shivery and a chance to do battle at sea on a whim. I asked if this barnacle infested mop bucket was up to the challenge. He slapped me on the back, as he laughed boastfully in my face with a true seamen's spirit, for I had stepped aboard the fastest clipper ship to ever sail the open seas. I replied jolly good then and ask he not spit in my face when he speaks. He then swiftly turned to his cabin boy, a man by the name of Turner and told him to fasten the sails, hoist the goose winged flying jib and set course at once for Manet's ship.

We were off in race with *A Fair Wind* catching the sails and a newfound confidence in the salty air that before the day was through, Botticelli would rue the day he ever painted my face into various shades and hues. Though I couldn't help but think, as we sailed away of all that I left behind. The girl I loved, a life I could have led and a life I once knew.

Though the winds were fair Manet's ship had the lead. It wasn't until the sun went down when we finally caught up to them. Raeburn and I went below to secure some paint, as Somerscales moved in for the kill. When we made it back up on deck, Botticelli had already struck his first blow with a stroke of yellow over the blueness of the ocean. I could barely make him out as he disappeared into a misty tunnel of chalky white smoke he created out of the clouds.

I scourged at him with a fist, that coward, but it was too late. The yellow oily hues from his palette unbound a strange current in the form of, *A Green Wave.*

It behaved like a wild, untamed animal. You could feel the sea shake and tremble. The wave slowly rose like a cat's paw arching over the ship, ready to pounce at any given moment. When the furry eyed beast reached the height of its summit, it bellowed a lunging scream. MEOW! That's when all hell broke loose. We were sucked right into the mouth of this foaming beast clawing and scratching at the sides of our vessel.

The wave then came back around for a second turn, roaring with viscosity. Raeburn held steady, waiting for the opportune moment. When the trough went under and the crest bounced back, he struck it with the brush and broke it in two. The wave scattered across the ocean, emeralds and jades streaming into the gulf, giving us a chance to go at it again.

The scene reminded me of a piece that once hung in our galleria, *The Sea Storm* and although the original artist never finished the painting, we commissioned another to finish were the other had left off. It was a fitting memory indeed for where Botticelli had left us in his dream.

While we were fending against the vivacious curves of a course and rigid sea who'd never known kindness or mercy, something unknown rammed into the side of the hull. Raeburn and I took a look overboard. I couldn't believe it, but there in the waters before us was a rather large tree, torn up from the roots no less. You would think, as great and vast and wide as the sea may appear to be, our captain, as great as he claimed to be, would have avoided it.

Raeburn was quick to action. He swiped the brush over its roots and steered it away. Moments later, the head of a monster, half beast, half tree burst free from this oily mess. I tell you the truth Fragonard. It was not just a mere sailors dream. We were now fighting two monsters, a wild and raging sea and an unnatural abomination of the forest.

The blood thirsty tree roared in anger, its branches snarling like tentacles. The stars in the sky were blotted out by a canopy of foliage.

Somerscales made a call to arms, "Load the cannons with everything we've got and fire at will towards the belly of the bark."

Turner and I loaded the cannons with bucket after bucket of paint and fired them right into the hollow of the oak. The tree gobbled them up and spit them back out, splattering paint all over the ocean, enchanting this mystical sea with every diabolical hue known to mortal man. Lightning flashed in pyres of red and orange, spiking in violets and yellows. We were facing an onslaught of hues, caught in the crosswinds of a mighty hurricane of colors.

The ship was swishing and swirling though mountain after mountain of oily waves. We trudged are way through as best we could. What a challenge it was with Somerscales at the helm and Raeburn, a true draftsmen of the sea with his knowledge of the color wheel. You know, you would never take the man for a painter, until he seizes the brush and palette in his hands. Honestly, I don't know what I would've done without their bravery.

When dawn approached the serpents pigments began to fade, but still it put up a good fight and so, we continued to fight back. The brush, however was no longer working in our defense. That's when we understood something about its magic, it only works at night. The only thing that truly did stop that horrid beast was daylight and a light mist of rain that fell over the ocean, washing away all the horrors Botticelli had unleashed.

I warn you, however, young Fragonard he has grown far more powerful since then. A light mist of rain will not stop his magic now, for it has become oil based.

With nothing but calm seas ahead we sailed on to Valparaiso. Our captain said he would tell tales of this epic battle for years to come, letting people know of our courage and of our bravery and how we had survived what would become known as, *The Greatest Storm.*

When we approached the waters *Off Valparaiso*, Somerscales found Manet's ship floating unattended. There was a rainbow of colors bleeding from the ocean waters, as if a gashing wound had been opened up. It was so odd. I'd never seen anything like it. The ship must have been carrying paintings of flowers and there were so many of them. It was like a garden eternally expanding in the sea.

Turner pointed out a shadowy figure, a mere image of a man trapped under the lapping waves of waterlilies. He said it was Manet's cabin boy and younger brother Monet. He recognized him because of his beard and mustache.

This mirage of a man, circum to such a horrific fate told us of how his brother was lost at sea. Botticelli threw him overboard for trying to start a mutiny. With the stroke of his brush, he turned him and their crew into strange looking fish for their actions of mutiny. He then painted himself into a bird with human hands and flew away. The poor soul than drifted into the abyss, as if Botticelli intended for him to only stay alive long enough to warn us of what would happen if we continued to hunt him down.

Somerscales and Turner offered up their services permanently to Raeburn and I for what Botticelli had done to their rivals. Turner took command of Manet's ship and Raeburn went with, in hopes that we might double our efforts. It looks like old Raeburn found him first and suffered the wrath of his artistic thoughts.

Before we parted ways he gave me this brush and told me to guard it with my life. Which I did and that is why I stand before you young Ayden, Prince and heir to the throne of the kingdom of Fragonard, in hopes that you will become our father's victors and end his reign of terror once and for all.

...And that was the end of his story and where mine truly began young Stefan.

XVI

SUNFLOWERS

"There must be something wrong with that coo, coo clock. It's gone off on another tantrum. Why that bird never seems to stop whistling, especially in the morning."

"Fragonard. The museum doesn't have a... never mind. So what happened next?"

"I know you would like to hear the rest, but it's getting late and nearing dawn. I'm awfully tired. Can't we continue this story another time?"

"Please. I have to know how it ends."

Fragonard yawned, "Oh, well I suppose I could stay up a little later tonight. I'm sure I can finish telling my story before the early morning bell begins to ring."

"That would be wonderful."

"Say, before I continue, why don't you fetch another painting for me to view."

"Alright, I'll go find one. Anything in particular?"

"No, not in particular. You pick one out again. I like the ones you find in that other room. You seem to have an eye for fine art."

"Okay, I'll see if I can find one to end the story."

Stefan wandered into the other room. He looked over the paintings and thought about the achievements of all those who had gone before him. Each one of these artists struggled in some way, yet overcame the odds and ended up hanging on the walls of this museum. The stories they could tell and the strokes behind the artists, if only they were animated like his friend in the painting.

Then he saw it, a double rainbow and it was beaming with bright colors. He knew Fragonard would love it, so he lifted the painting off the wall and brought it back to him.

"Fragonard, look what I found."

"You do have a way with picking out the most exquisite paintings. Such wonderful subject matter. I absolutely adore this piece. It's breathtaking. Who painted it and what is the name of this masterpiece. I must know."

"It's called *The Blind Girl*, by John Everett Millais."

"Oh I do hope someday they'll hang me up in that other room. I look forward to seeing what else they have over there."

"Hey, Fragonard."

"Yes, young Stefan."

"While I was over there I was thinking about something."

"Well, what is it? We don't have all night to stand around and talk about it. The sun will be up soon and I do have some things I must be getting too."

"I was wondering. Do you really think I've got what it takes to one day become a great painter like one of these artists?"

"Of course I do. All it takes is hard work and a little bit of effort if you want to achieve your dreams. Just like Van Gogh and Seurat. Not to forget to mention Thomas Benton, Millet, Homer, Degas, Lebrun and all the other great painters you've set in front of me for me to view."

"How will I know if I've worked hard enough like them?"

Fragonard cleared the oils in his throat and spoke with great wisdom as he often did.

"The poet's pen is the poet's truth, for if the poet dies, than the poet's dream must have become real."

"I'm not sure if I understand."

"What I'm trying to say young Stefan, is the stars are still out there, swirling in soft and lightly colored patches of blue, the way Van Gogh intended when his brush moved across the canvas. Find those stars and when you do, don't give up on them. It would be a shame if you let the dust settle before your dreams fade on the canvas as will I one day."

"I think I understand."

"I suppose now I should continue with my story."

"No, wait. There's one more painting I wanted to show you. I'll be right back with it and then you can continue."

In the other corner of the room there was a painting Stefan had been looking at when he first heard Fragonard's voice.

Fragonard shifted his eyes and said, "You're not going to get one from the other room?"

Stefan pulled the painting off the wall and said, "I thought this one would be better to end the story with. It's my second favorite painting in the museum. I always look at when I come here."

He then carried the painting over to the others and set it in the middle of the pile.

Fragonard's eyes lit up, "Oh Stefan. It's like a strike of inspiration beaming over the horizon. I must ask, how long has this painting been hanging next to me?"

"I have no idea, but I stop and look at it every time I come to the museum."

"Those are some beautiful sunflowers. Van Gogh did an outstanding job. I can almost smell them from here. It really brightens this room. Holbein would have loved them, if he were still around."

"I'm sure of it. So can I hear the rest of your story now?"

"Oh yes. Speaking of which, where did I leave off? I was in the midst of telling you of Bordone's part in this whole thing. You know, I gave you the short version of his tale. Listening to him babble on about himself and his royal standing with the king often put me to sleep."

"Well, let me see if I can remember? Oh yeah... He just got done from a long voyage at sea. You were still chained to the wall next to his friend and I think he was just about to finish with the rest of his story."

"Ah yes, I remember now and things took an interesting turn at quite the odd angle."

Stefan sat down on the bench with two fingers and a thumb pressed against the sides of his chin and listened to the rest of his story.

XVII

THE ALGEBRAIC

EQUATION OF A MADMAN

Though Bordone held the key to my freedom, there were still a few questions that went unanswered. I had to know, so I asked.

"Bordone, how exactly did you find me then?"

"After about a year or so of chasing stories of Botticelli's magic from town to town, led by the ever changing stars above, I arrived in the outskirts of your village. On my walk through your countryside, I ran into a man who had gotten his cart stuck in a black oily mire. I helped him get back on his feet. He seemed like an ornery buffoon, nodding his head and grunting a lot. After he brushed himself off, he introduced himself to me as Grant Wood of the once hardworking kingdom of Fragonard. Before we parted ways he told me your story."

"And your father, did you ever find him?"

"Unfortunately so. I showed up in town just in time to watch as Botticelli set my father and all of your kingdoms creative efforts to a flame. It was a most horrific site. One I will never forget nor forgive him for."

"I'm sorry for your loss. I wish there was something more I could do."

"It's too late for that now. The important thing is that we find a way to save Raeburn and see to it your father's fate does not end up the same as mine."

"Don't worry, we will. So how did you manage to break through to the dungeon? I'm going to need a way to escape this cell, once you paint these chains off of me."

"It was not an easy task. I thought I'd never find you. Then late one evening, as I was taking a stroll around the courtyard a sinkhole opened up and presented itself to me and so I took my advantage. Oh by the way, there were these gigantic oily worms I had to avoid on the way in. No doubt apart of Botticelli's magic and attempts to maintain his flowerbed."

"Yes, I'm sure that's the reason for them."

"Tell me Fragonard, do you believe you possess the skills necessary to defeat him once and for all?"

"I do. Now paint me free from these chains Bordone, so that I may get that chance to do honorable and noble battle with an unjust man."

Bordone painted me free from the chains that had held me back since Botticelli's arrival. He then handed me the brush and what little paint he carried with. Before I left his side, he gave me a few parting words to help aid me in my final duel with Botticelli.

"Take this knowledge with you before you leave this night. The skills of the brush only work by painting on objects that already exist and its magic will only work under the light of the moon. So if you are still in the midst of your duel when the sun begins to rise, be sure to choose wisely what you decide to paint. Now go, young Fragonard and come back to this cell when you are through with him as our father's victors."

The brush only working under the light of the moon was something I didn't know before. I was grateful for the advice he gave me. I promised Bordone I would come back as our father's victors and restore his Picasso of a face back to normal. I then left him weeping by Raeburn's side as I started crawling my way through the dirt and the mud to the surface, so I could begin the fight of my life.

When I reached the courtyard I noticed the trellis leading up to a balcony bubbling out from the castle. If I was to defeat him I needed a way to get inside and find where my father and the kingdom's paint were being stored.

Before I could even take a step, my signature on the courtyard winked and then blew me a kiss, stolen from her granite lips. I thought my eyes were playing tricks on my imagination, until she stepped down from her pedestal. I tried to go around, then her friend got down off her pedestal and batted an eyelash my way. It was Lavina and Scultori, my old crushes from when I was young. I politely asked if I could pass, but alas, it was of no use. After all, they were but mere statues.

I was stuck in a stone cold gaze, frozen in time with a question mark appropriately placed above my head. I couldn't find a single flaw in either one of them. Not a loose crevasse, crack or seam was showing, nor telling for that matter. Lavina twirled her fingers through her curly locks of hair, as if though I were interested. Scultori then blew me a kiss, sealing it with her own dreamy desires. The two of them began arguing over which hand I would take in marriage or at least an innocent stroll around the courtyard. I was caught in the middle, between a rock and a hard place quite literally.

Lavina swayed the running strikes of her contouring lines like she owned the world, held in the palm of her hands down to the smallest of details. I tried to reason with her. To let her know it wouldn't be fair to the other if I simply went out with her sister. She punched me in the shoulder as hard as she could. I cried, "Ouch, that hurts!" but she didn't seem to care whether or not she left a mark.

I'd finally lost my breath over these two maidens of the garden that kept the flowers in bloom all year long. I thought perhaps another night then, but my father awaited me in the castle to paint things right. So I looked away with the thought of what could have been and climbed up the trellis.

When I set foot on the balcony I had to sit down, for an amazing transformation had taken place inside the castle. I stared down an unusual hallway with gradual changes leading into something of a more complex nature.

It went on and on for as long as the eye would allow it. The walls on either side were made of sky and water. The ceilings were even more bizarre, resting high and low, close and far away, depending on where and how you looked at it. It had a black and white prism of eye catching illusions, set in movements on a linoleum cut floor, unbound by the natural laws of physics.

Just inside the window, resting in the corners laying flat on the floor was a nest of *Dormant Butterflies.* It was as if they were waiting on someone to come along and disturb their slumber, so they could show me a new perspective to catch one's imagination off guard.

I stepped into the floor and inadvertently unleashed a cluttered storm of rhombuses, isotopic triangles and pentagonal tiling's. Liberated from their placid, geometric design, the butterflies sprawled out like a spider web, taking flight, *Dividing and Developing* into new forms. I ran down the hallway, chasing these fluttering illusions further out of my sights, making a game of it. They flew up the walls and then trickled back down from the wallpaper one by one, dropping and stacking on top of each other, squeezing into an acute symmetry of equilateral proportions.

I joyfully kept playing with them, until I stubbed my toe on a funny looking caterpillar with a mind complex.

"Get out of here, you dam! bug." I shamed its behavior.

The caterpillar turned its head completely around, then it curled up by using its hands and feet. I flicked the little critter with my finger for being such a rude bugger.

The caterpillar rolled off in a zig-zagging motion, which caused a chain-reaction to happen. The angles of the hallway started to splice and interlock. The butterflies turned into insects. The insects turned into birds and the birds turned into lizards which ate the butterflies and it all must have started from that first step I took on the floor when I entered the castle that night.

I'd wandered into a Pythagorean of enigmas. I lost my bearing, my sense of direction, time and space inside a vertex of improper fractions and inconsistent variables. The pattern was perplexing, absurdly obtuse even. There was no predestination to this *Tetrahedral Planetoid.* It was *Order then Chaos, Order then Chaos* planned in some sort of carefully conceived ill-rational manner.

It was then that I realized the hallway worked in phases like a game of chess, linear lines, coordinates set on a grid. There was an order of operations here and if I wanted to find the hypotenuse, I had to follow it precisely. Now if only I could find one line that was parallel to another that did not change direction when I stared into its depths for too long. Then I might stand a chance of finding out where it all met up in the end.

Just when I thought I knew exactly where I was headed the lines started to form a curve, metamorphosing into a spherical shape, controlled by two intercepting planes leading into the floor. The two planes interlocked, coiling in a whirlpool effect, allowing me to pierce into a one sided fishbowl. I tapped on the glass, the floor in response instantly became *Smaller and Smaller*, reducing the diameter of its circumference to the square root of its limits. When I stopped to focus in, the lines of this pattern slowly faded back into place.

When I tapped on the glass a second time, a hyperbolic wave pushed towards the center. Then rippled back across, spiraling out in an algorithm, reaching a quantum of endless probabilities. The knowns, the unknowns and the truly unknown, unknowns.

I had to unravel the mystery behind this *Concentric Rind* soon or circum to its inner depth. But alas, it seemed I was trapped forever in the algebraic equation of a madman, who hid all his best kept secrets within the perpendicular lines of this black and white dream palace of sorts.

I stepped passed the whirlpool and continued further down the hall, until I came upon a door. I put my hand on the handle and entered a strange loop, a fractal dimension. Its architecture built upon *Impossible Construction*. The design behind it looked like a print gallery, a place for Botticelli to practice the future of his art. It was a library of infinite possibilities, progressive anthological formulas, categorized and indexed with astounding precision.

It appeared he was going through a transitional phase and I was left to search through corridor after corridor in this Escher like maze of his.

Stairs ran rampant, *Up and Down, Ascending and Descending*. The ceilings looked like walls, the walls looked like ceilings and the floor, was nowhere to be found. There was no *Relativity* to this *House of Stairs* made of *Waterfalls*. The only question was, how would I know where I was going if I did not get there first and which way did it all really lead? I had to start somewhere. You very well can't get anywhere if you feel you're going nowhere.

I walked down which led up. I walked up which led sideways. It was a jester and a jackals game. I guess I may never truly know where I stood that night in Botticelli's room of lost perspective points.

I ended up somewhere in the middle of where this had all started. It was then that I realized there was a repeating pattern at every interval, every scale down to the smallest of details. There were logical truths to this room after all, where one finds oneself where one started off, a picture appearing within itself repetitively if you will.

So I tried not to climb this mountain of stairs by stepping on what was below me, but instead I pulled myself up from what was above. This endless *Cycle of Stairs* then just all of a sudden simply fell apart under the weight of its own perception and I was on my way to the next paradox in this impossible puzzle box.

This led me to another world of mind numbing mathematics, a geometric room lost in the concept of perception. It was a place unlike any other I had seen in the castle. The stars and heavens above made up the walls of this *Other World*. There were astrological signs, maps, graphs and charts, perhaps coordinates to newborn stars. Was he a pessimist, optimist unsure of the truth? It didn't add up. He was searching for something, but what? One thing for certain, time kept aware of him as much as he was aware of it.

There was a drafting table with sketches of geometric shapes, a *Study for the Stars*. Next to the table was an astronomer's telescope. I peered into its lens, hoping to catch a glimpse into this dreary dream world Botticelli had surrounded himself in. What I saw was a bird with eight human heads staring into an empty plane of existence. It was perhaps the only creature in this world that could look at it and truly comprehend what was going on. Though, from what I've come to learn appearances can be deceiving.

The next room appeared to be empty as well and lead to nowhere in particular, at least visible to the naked eye. I looked back from where I came, only to discover a wall was in its place. I had walked right into a *Blind Man's Bluff* set up by Botticelli, meant to deceive anyone who made it this far in his Escher like maze.

I had survived his *Three Worlds*. His *Black and White Labyrinth of Insanity* and the lines attributed to his mosaic of *Day and Night*. It all came together in the end, truly reflecting the *Rippled Surface* of his tortured soul. Now all I had to do was figure out how to put this *Knotted Rubrics Cube* back together with a lock and no key.

There were two hands drawing themselves to life on the wall. I wondered if they would put down their pencils and point the way. I asked, but the answer I got made the least amount of sense. One pointed in one direction and the other in the opposite way. I should have known, for the hands after all drew upon this madness, thriving upon its indifference to the calculations presented.

Though the room did appear to be empty, hidden from view was a magic mirror. It reflected things more like a sphere, refracting the images of what appeared on the other side around it. I tilted the mirror slightly and noticed a doorway to another room, possibly another world, standing adjacent to where I stood. I now knew one of these walls in this eight-sided-box had to be a ruse or a mobius strip if you will. Appearing to be flat on the surface, though in reality holding great truths to its deception.

After inspecting my surroundings by a divisible measure, I noticed one of the walls that was pixilated, separating it from the rest. It had a mezzotint to it, white lines littered over blackened steps. I stepped forth and it opened up, revealing the *Vaulted Staircase* that led where my father was being kept.

Once in this room of reality that added to a sum, I walked up to my father's portrait and looked into his fading eyes. He was still quite ill and coughing profusely. I promised I would defeat Botticelli, then return to paint him free him from the confines of the canvas with the bristles on the end of my new brush. He was proud to know I hadn't given into Botticelli's lies. He told me to keep my head held high and to not treat him the way he treated us, for a Fragonard carries a noble brow lifted high on their side. I assured him I would on my honor as a hardworking Prince and humble servant of the people.

I didn't have time to waste, so I painted the magic lock off the door where the kingdom's paint was being stored. Then I laid it all out before me in a circle and started mixing up a palette worthy enough to combat against Botticelli's egocentric nature. There was every color of the rainbow in my arsenal you could think of. Midnight blue, fiery orange, rosy red, Verde green, cadmium yellow, a plethora of violets and purples and many other shades and hues.

When the work was through I turned to my father and told him I would return to his side by the time the sun rose over our once glorious fields, free from his magic and his treachery. Then I climbed out the window, ready to begin the battle of my life with wet paint dripping from my brush.

On the walk through town I could still here Lavina and Scultori arguing over me in the courtyard. I knew their battle was an epic one indeed, worthy enough to be written down in a love letter sent to the heavens above, but the battle between me and Botticelli was going to be something that may very well shape the entire universe and determine its fate from then on.

Things had changed, yet stayed the same in our humble little kingdom. The town had become a dark and dismal place, void of light or hope. The homes were sketched out in graphite. The roads, partially paved in a wash of dirty brown and charcoal. I remember walking passed the grand row of trees Botticelli painted on either side of the main road leading up to the castle. They were no longer lush and full of green character, fit for the birds that used to nest in them, but morbid and empty, just like Botticelli.

When I made it to the edge of town I found a vine hanging down from the castle walls. I latched on and climbed my way up. At the top I looked out into a world beaming with color and hope. Botticelli had turned our once meager fields into his fabled island, his depiction of a dream palace of sorts, shared only by his callous thoughts.

There he was in the distance, on top of a hill resting before another, sleeping underneath the shade of that tree he was so fond of. Near him was the tree stump he'd helped me to remove from the fields. Surrounding the two hills was his world of strange and surreal oddities he painted to make himself feel at home in our kingdom. The trees with leaves made up of many different shapes and shades. Dotted all over the landscape were the pools of mystical colors he so fondly talked about. Rocks everywhere seemed to randomly get up from their spots and walk away. It truly was a beautiful dream. Though it was not his own, he masterfully borrowed it.

I knew I couldn't battle him on his own terms, for his terms were unjust. No, I couldn't let him sleep so comfortably in our kingdom anymore. I decided to even the odds by painting this dream of his to a more fitting place to do battle. The place where it all began, in the fields. So I went to wake him from his dream and let his nightmare finally begin with the stroke of my brush.

222

XVIII

THE MASTERS DUEL

I walked up and over the first hill and then up and over the other to where Botticelli lay under the shade of that tree he was so fond of. I wasn't about to give my first blow while he was still asleep in a starry daze. I made my intentions well known by kicking dirt in his eyes, asking he get up from his deceitful slumber and face me, for unlike him I had nobility and honor on my side.

He slowly woke from his dream with a startled, bewildering look, as though he couldn't believe that I stood before him on top of that hill.

"What's this foul taste you've put in my mouth?" he coughed and complained.

With a passionate gusto, I veered in his face, "That dirt is a badge of honor for those who have learned to work hard for their efforts."

Botticelli folded his hat over his eyes and propped himself back up against the tree.

"Let's continue this unpleasant conversation another time Fragonard. I was just in the middle of a rather pleasant..."

I kicked another pile of dirt on him, and then I gestured with a hand, "I suggest you wipe the crust from your eyes, for the dream you thought you were in, is now under my command."

My words with him were quite smug indeed. That's when he noticed his dream world had become a representation of the one thing he loathed more than anything else in life. Hard backbreaking labor and the efforts of a true master of the plow.

"My azaleas. They're ruined and the geraniums. You've turned them into alfalfa sprouts. Yuck! How were you able to do this?"

"It just so happens that I too have a magic paintbrush, given to me by a man by the name of Ethan Bordone and crafted under the masterful skills of his dear old friend Raeburn."

He responded in a violent rage, "You do not choose to battle with me boy! I am Jared Botticelli, masterful painter and daydreamer."

I swung the brush viciously in the air behind me, my palate held at an angle as a shield in my defense, "Now we shall see who is the true master Botticelli, once and for all."

With a vengeful glint gleaming in his eyes, reflecting in my own, he pulled out his brush and palette.

"Very well young Fragonard. If you wish to continue with this absurd duel, then let's see what you've really got."

The battle began with a stroke of red and brown paint, as he transformed the tree into a horrid beast. The branches became animated and started hurling its limbs at me. I responded with glee in my heart, as I pulled a lighting bolt out of the sky, splitting the tree in two. The ground shook and rumbled with a thunderous roar that lit up the air around us.

"The gloves are off for this fight. You will no longer find a tree to give you shade while you sleep the day away in my kingdom." I proudly championed.

With that crooked smile of his lifted, he backed up from my deadly flame and said,

"End this *Useless Resistance* to my skill and I'll spare your life, allowing you to live the rest of your days as a blade of grass in this field."

I grinned with a brow raised against his, strong in will and determination. "Noble gesture old man, but before this night is through I will see to it you are paid full value for that debt you are owed for the work you put in."

Now it was my turn and what, I wondered, would be fitting for my first attempt to put him in his place. Then I saw it swirling above me, moving in-between the stars in lightly colored patches of blue. I released the power of the winds, sending gust after gallant gust after him. Botticelli held his ground quite fiercely for an old man. His hat even almost blew away, yet he still managed to keep it on his head.

Then his face lit up with a smirking grin, as if it was going to be easy to do away with my innocent dream. He dipped his brush into a darkened corner of the night and painted a thousand bats free from the wickedness of his thoughts. Their wings expanded and contracted, quickly turning the tides against me.

I'll admit, it was a creative effort on his part, something I hadn't expected, but wit was my advantage, a skill I now possessed. I pulled an apple from out of my pocket and painted it a set of pearly white chompers. Then I presented it before him as a passing test of my proven right to wield the brush. The bats quickly took the bait and the apple swallowed them whole, bite after bite.

Botticelli scowled, "Tell me Fragonard, how are you able to come up with such an imaginative dream, when all you've ever known is how to tend to the chores?"

"It is but a mere parlor trick, a small taste of what I can really do. Like the one you used to deceive me with the apple long ago, when we should have been working hard in those fields."

"You couldn't have possibly learned it all from tilling the earth and breaking your back with a shovel."

This concept of earning one's reward before enjoying the fruits of your labor was clearly lost on him. So I came clean and told him the truth.

"If you must know. Night after night I borrowed your brush. While you were snoring under a blanket of stars I practiced on my own surrounded by a bed of your dreams, until I learned how to wield the brush proper like a master."

Botticelli scorned, "You'll pay for riffling through my things."

We then began dueling again, tit for tat, back and forth, with a swab and a jab at the ego as we fought it out over the two hills.

"Tell me Botticelli, why did you scar Bordone's face? Is there a reason for your atrocity?"

Botticelli swung as I parried and said, "The bumbling fool, with his child like paintings. He led a life living in the shadow of his father's, not knowing the whole time their was a world out there just waiting to be conquered."

"That is a dream of your buffoonery alone and an unjust one at that." I said, as I swung at him in an attempt to swipe that crooked smile off his lips.

"You can't enjoy pie without breaking the crust." He retorted.

I stomped my foot on the ground, my brush thrusting forward, "What about Raeburn, couldn't handle the competition?"

That comment really seemed to send him over the edge. So I swiped the brush at his feet and cut the grass out from under him. He slipped back and fell over the tree stump. I offered to help him on his feet, a gesture of good intent extended in the heat of battle. Instead, he did the most dastardly thing. He threw a pile of dirt in my face, ungrateful for the gracious living my kingdom had provided for him.

While I was brushing myself off, it gave him enough time to come back with a masterful feat. He swirled his brush into the clouds, releasing a down pour of rain. Every color of the rainbow fell from the sky, scattering across the landscape.

I painted a ditch to let the water drain so we could both catch our breath. I stood on one side wearing my well worn garments and he stood on the other, with another trick up his finely woven sleeve.

"Had enough old man?" I said, as I swatted the brush side to side.

"Not by a long shot. Let's see if you can top this trick with the eye. You'll never truly understand the concept of perspective points."

He then held up his thumb and wielded his brush in the opposite direction near our village.

In an instant he was gone. Poof! Vanished into the distance of the perspective zone. I couldn't let it end there. I tapped the brush behind me, causing the hilltop to rise in a swell. I kept building up speed, until I landed right back at his deceitfully crooked smile.

Just before this mountain of earth came crashing down, I yelled in triumph, "Is this the perspective you were looking for?"

"Worthy attempt Fragonard, but I have to ask, are you humble enough to step down off your throne or do you prefer to wrestle around in the mud like a pig?"

I suppose I could have ignored his request and left it at that, but I accepted his challenge to keep the balance of things well in proportion.

Once on the streets, Botticelli backed up with palette in hand and that awful crooked grin of his and so we started dueling again. I told him it was his turn to lay down a stroke and to lap it on thick with a fresh coat of paint.

He smeared his brush across his palette and then swiped it over a bed of daffodils. The flowers became animated and sprung to life. I was shrouded in a haze of glittery dust. So I painted a pebble free from the road. The stone hopped up and started bashing the butterflies, splattering them all over his well crafted cobbled streets.

Lavina and Scultori then broke through the garden walls and brought their brawl in the courtyard into the middle of our fight. I said if he was not careful, I would turn their lust for my fair hair into a lust for his oily blood.

Botticelli let out a mocking laugh, "If you expect me to believe you created a woman, let alone two of impeccable beauty, then I shall create a man with a well chiseled chin for the two of them to swoon over instead."

With the stroke of his brush, he turned that stone in mid hop into a man with dashing good looks. Goliath stomped his foot on the ground and then he strolled away arm and arm with the two loves of my life. All I could think of is what a horrible trick to play on such a dear old friend. That's when I noticed he'd taken this advantage with another skill he possessed, to run off from his dreams. I thought to myself, what a coward not to finish what he'd started.

I boastfully shouted, "Where are you going? You still haven't seen a true test of my skill played out yet this night on the streets you claim to have provided for the peoples knotted feet."

I couldn't let him escape, not after that dastardly blow to my heart. So I made a dash to Landseer's to end this night standing on all fours. When I arrived I noticed the lock had been picked. The door then burst open and Botticelli rode passed me.

I yelled out, "Curse you Botticelli and the preponderance of your arrogance. We shall see who wins the night and who is asleep when the sun rises over those two hills you undeservingly rest your back on."

That's exactly what was on his mind. He rode back out to the fields as he prepared himself for his last grand and epic feat. I jumped on a horse and rode after him. I was dogging and dashing his blows, until finally he nailed a good one and knocked me off my horse. Botticelli threw everything he could at me. I was a *Cart Stuck in the Mire* with a broken axle and no one around to give me a helping hand and pull me out. So I used what he threw at me and turned it into a dream of my own by painting my greatest feat yet.

There I stood tall on a mountain top made of soil, as he proclaimed he was finally done with me and my trickery.

"You could have been my apprentice young Ayden, Prince and heir to the throne of a pile of dirt, but you lack the skills necessary to be a masterful painter. Now you will rue the day you ever crossed paths with me, Jared Botticelli, master of the brush!"

Botticelli released the magic of the stars, a trick he learned from me when we first met. Thousands of them hurled toward the earth in a shower of hell fire and rain, but this time I didn't swipe them away. With what little wit remained on the tip of my brush I painted the mountain of dirt into a pile of unstable rocks. The stars pounded into the side of the hill and tore it to smithereens.

Sparks flickered and dirt shot into the air, as Botticelli and I fell away from the mountain. There were no more tricks up his sleeve and unlike him I had the upper hand all along, because before the battle even began I'd painted my brush and palette firmly to my hands.

I dug myself out and stood over him, ready for his last and final words. He claimed mercy be shown, but I wasn't about to be merciful when a thought occurred to me for a fitting end to his treachery. I dipped my brush into a bit of white paint and just before the sun rose, I painted poor Botticelli into the sky as a cloud and watched as he drifted away, never to be seen ever again.

After the battle I painted myself free from the brush and palette and walked back to our village, which seemed to return to normal, as his curse had been lifted and his dream had floated away along with him into the clouds.

I returned to my father's humble little home and what a relief it was, Enstrom and his daughter, Renoir, Bordone and Raeburn were waiting there for me. I couldn't help but think of the absence of Grant Wood and Logan Landseer. The part those two played in this tale truly left a hole in my heart and in our kingdom, which would not be so easily filled. As if it ever could be filled without the help of Grant Wood and Landseer's skills.

When night fell I painted Raeburn a face and put the proportions of Bordone's back into place, yet there was still one lingering scar on his cheek I couldn't seem to swipe away. He asked that I leave him this mark, as a reminder of what Botticelli had done to him and his father. I now had to paint my father back to health, which was an easy thing to do, but painting him free from the canvas proved to be impossible. It seemed he was bound to the oils for all eternity, as if there was no way of breaking this last and final lingering spell. I sighed in distress, but alas, it was a part of Botticelli's magic he took with him when he floated away.

I sat down on the bench outside our home with my head in my hand. Bordone sat down next to me to try and cheer me up. He told me of the night Botticelli painted his father onto the canvas. He said something strange happened when he leaned in to give him a hug. A part of him traded places with his father for but a moment. He then leaned back and noticed his hands, they had broken free from the oils on the canvas. He wasn't sure if this would help, but I now knew what I would have to do to break this curse and I knew it was something my father would just have to live with for the rest of his life.

I walked into my father's home and leaned into the portrait to give him a hug and tell him that I loved him and that I would do anything for him, no matter the cost. We held for a final warm embrace, before I traded places with him inside this canvas, forever sealing my fate and that is how I stand before you this night young Stefan, trapped in this painting for all eternity.

My father was heartbroken, but so was I. For all that I had put him through, put our kingdom through. I refused to leave the painting and ordered the brushes to be burned at once until there was nothing left, so that this horrific fate could never befall upon anyone or any kingdom ever again. My father begged I reconsider, but I contested. Eventually, he accepted my fate and did as I said. He threw the two brushes into the fireplace and I watched them burn from within the confines of this canvas.

Something mystical happened, as I watched the brushes smolder into ash. The flames lit up, sparkling in many different shades and hues. There was, let me see... Every color of the rainbow. Red and green, blue and pink, orange and purple. This nightmarish black soot flowed endlessly from the tips of these surreal flames. They began to take on a life of their own, dancing around my father's fireplace, as if playing one last final game for my amusement. A fitting end, for the secret to this magic was not meant to be squandered on human hands ever again.

Something else strange happened, I swear to you young Stefan. I saw a pair of soft yellow eyes staring right back at me in content, as the last of these colorful flames dwindled away in my father's fireplace.

Bordone and Raeburn decided to stay on as field hands in our kingdom. They never returned to their homeland. It took some doing for my father to get them used to our way of life. Working with a shovel and coming home every night with dirt on their backs wasn't their forte. After a couple of years though, I'll say this. They finally found their niche and truly earned the right to wear the dirt in our fields as a badge of honor for the work they put in.

Once they found their niche they were even able to find some time to paint a few things here and there. They would often leave their works of art in my father's home for my critique. My father, he eventually got used to having a son hang up on his wall. I have a lot of fond memories in that humble little home of ours as a painting.

Years later Grant Wood returned to our kingdom. My father couldn't have been happier to have him around and so was I. Of course, Logan Landseer was never forgotten. A statue was commissioned by my father in his honor.

I remember the day well when newcomers started visiting our kingdom again. My father was out in the fields working hard tending to the crops and the chores that so desperately needed to get done, when a young man showed up outside our home. He must not have known I was a painting, as I appeared to be just fine from the view in the window.

I looked at him with a brow raised and said, "Halt, who goes there?"

He humbly replied, "The name is Pettie. I heard your kingdom accepts people from other nations and well, I was looking for work."

"My name is Ayden and I am Prince and heir to the throne of the kingdom of Fragonard. We are always open to those from other nations who can no longer support themselves in their homeland, for whatever reason it is they have. You may stay in the kingdom of Fragonard for as long as you like, so long as you like to farm or raise goats. That is, unless you have any special skills or talents our kingdom could use."

"I used to be a stable boy back home, but they have plenty of those. There's just no work for me there."

"There is a seat open at a stable not far from here. I warn you however, the man who once worked there, his shoes will not be easy to fill. The job is yours though, but only if you are willing to work hard for your meal at the end of the day."

Author Bio: The author of The Magic Paintbrush currently lives in the land beyond, beyond, a place past hope and fear where only dreamers dare to exist in defiance of all we know as reality. It is a place between here and nowhere.

YA artistic-fantasy. The world's most famous
painters battle it out over control of...

THE MAGIC PAINTBRUSH

Ayden Fragonard, the boy in the painting recounts
his tale and his tragedy.

My tale begins over 550 years ago. I was a Prince
back then working my father's fields, tending to the
daily chores. We didn't have much, but enough to
earn a humble living. I had no idea what a dream was
or could be. All I knew how to do was work a plough
and milk a goat, skills that are perfectly useless. I'm
still not really sure how a plough works?

Newcomers started arriving in the spring as they did
every year. I met a painter by the name of Jared
Botticelli. I was infatuated by this man's talents with
the brush. My father wanted me to go back to work
in the fields. I should've listened to him. Once I had
the brush in hand though, I could never go back to
my plain, boring farming life. The thrill of painting
was in my blood.

This brush could do almost anything. It could bring
inanimate objects to life, like turning flowers into
butterflies, trees into monsters and tattoos into paint
breathing dragons. It could do almost anything, but
release me from my fate. That is why I stand before
you hanging on the wall in this museum, trapped in
this painting many years later telling you my story. I
hope in some way my tale will help you with a dream
that your father just doesn't understand.